The boat tossed like a bottle on the sea!

Standing there, buffeted by the wind and half deafened by the noise of the waves, Jo watched the tiny lifeboat slowly work its way out to sea. And she realized suddenly that the boat held the one person who meant everything in the world to her.

Her hand sought Hannah's as she prayed. She was not alone; other women in the silent crowd had men in the lifeboat, as well.

Hannah's words came unbidden into her mind. "The sea's his life, not his living. If you can't accept it, leave Dan alone, or it'll end in misery for both of you."

Jo wondered if she had the strength to do either....

D0669387

OTHER
Harlequin Romances
by SUE PETERS

1850—THE STORM WITHIN
1874—DESIGN FOR DESTINY
1916—WHEELS OF CONFLICT
1959—DEEP FURROWS
1975—CLOUDED WATERS
2030—ONE SPECIAL ROSE
2104—PORTRAIT OF PARADISE
2156—LURE OF THE FALCON

Entrance to the Harbour

by

SUE PETERS

Harlequin Books

TORONTO • LONDON • NEW YORK • AMSTERDAM
SYDNEY • HAMBURG • PARIS

Original hardcover edition published in 1978
by Mills & Boon Limited

ISBN 0-373-02204-2

Harlequin edition published October 1978

CHAPTER ONE

'CAN'T we go back home, Jo?'

'This is home, from now on, Chris.'

It did not look much like it. Jo Wallace pulled the collar of her scarlet poplin mac closer about her ears, and wondered why she had bothered to tie a scarf over her hair. Both were irretrievably soaked. And the grey stone cottage confronting them, with its slate roof shining with rain, offered no immediate prospect of warmth to dry out. She shivered.

'It looks sort of—cold, doesn't it?' Spaniel brown eyes turned up towards hers in mute appeal, and the faint tremor in the young voice, instantly stifled, rallied her own failing courage as nothing else could have done.

'It'll be all right as soon as we get a fire going,' she answered him brightly, trying to convince herself as much as the boy. The cottage not only looked cold, it looked inhospitable. Hostile, almost. I'm getting over-imaginative, she scolded herself, and impulsively reached down for her brother's hand. 'Come on, let's get inside out of this rain. Where did I put the key?' The brief human contact added a further boost to her determination, and she pushed open the rickety garden gate that led up a weed-strewn path to the front door, fumbling in her bag while trying hard not to wish that their inheritance had been one of the cottages that flanked the steep cobbled street of St Mendoc. The little houses in the village stood cheek by jowl, jostling one another for space, and without the amenity of a garden such as this one boasted, but at least they were a part of the bustling fishing community, and did not stand lonely and aloof as the one that confronted them did, clinging limpet-like to the cliff edge that made a peremptory boundary to the wild garden.

'It's dark inside.' Chris stood on tiptoe and rubbed his finger against the bottom pane of the window, making a small squeaking sound in the mist-shrouded silence.

'That's because of the mist. It'll be bright enough as soon as the sun comes out, I expect. This rain won't last,' she told him, with more hope than confidence. 'It's a good job we're not rich,' she added ruefully. 'We'll have no need to lock the door when we go out. I can hardly turn this thing.' She brought both hands to bear on the large, old-fashioned key. It yielded to the extra pressure reluctantly, with a grating sound that made her make a mental note to acquire some oil as soon as possible. 'Welcome ho——' The screech of the door hinges stopped her in mid-sentence, and she and her brother looked at one another in silence. The hinges needed an application of lubricant as badly as the lock, and their banshee groan added to the unwelcoming appearance of the cottage itself, enhanced by an icy draught of air from the tiny living room inside that smelled musty from damp and long disuse.

'I don't want to stay here, Jo. I don't like it.' The beginnings of mutiny showed in the thin pale face below her shoulder, and Jo hardened her heart, trying not to see his limp as her brother turned towards her, his features so like her own, with his brown eyes topped by soft brown wavy hair, that they might have been looking in a mirror. His face was tight with the tension she had learned to dread, and had hoped would go away for good when they came to St Mendoc.

'Dad and Mother wouldn't have bought the place as a holiday cottage if they didn't like it. And thought we'd like it too.' Deliberately she spoke of her parents as she would have done if they had still been alive. 'And you don't like it because you've always been used to brown stone buildings,' she pointed out practically. 'The grey granite tends to look cold, but we'll soon change all that. A lick of bright paint...'

Still talking, she stepped through the door, relying on Chris to follow her automatically. The sound of his uneven footsteps on the bare board floor told her she had guessed correctly. 'Now, where's the fuel kept, I wonder? I think Mother said there was some in a bunker by the scullery door. Look around,' she bade the boy briskly, 'the sooner we find it the sooner we'll get a fire going in that grate.' She regarded the old-fashioned hearth in a corner of the sparsely furnished living room with some misgivings, and hoped the chimney did not need sweeping. 'I want a cup of tea,' she declared thirstily, 'and something to eat. And then we'll have to see about getting the blankets and sheets aired.' Her heart contracted as she spoke, but she had her back turned towards Chris, and he could not see her face. The cottage was fully equipped. Their parents had brought everything down for the holiday they never had. The holiday on which Jo was to have joined them a week later, and for which they had set out in the car gaily enough with Chris, on the journey that ended with an accident that left Jo and her brother orphaned, and the ten-year-old boy fighting a battle to walk again.

With indomitable courage, and the resilience of childhood, he won, but of the two Jo had the harder battle. To her fell the task of removing the family belongings from the Don's House, the cosy, brown stone lodge traditionally occupied by the Professor of History at the ancient seat of learning that had been her father's natural home. His gentle, scholarly presence pervaded every room, and eventually, her task completed, Jo found she was glad to leave. Even glad to turn her back on the familiar town filled with bicycle-riding students who wove dangerously in and out of the traffic in the narrow streets, with flying gowns and cheerful banter, and welcomed Jo to all their functions with happy camaraderie. Melvin resented their easy friendliness, but then Melvin was jealous of anyone who occupied Jo's attention.

'This looks like a fuel bunker.' Chris forgot his trepidation in the interest of exploring, and signalled his sister triumphantly. Since losing their parents, Jo had felt glad she was fifteen years older than her brother. At least it gave him someone he could turn to, someone close. Melvin had been close—or she thought he had. Resolutely she thrust the thought of Melvin from her mind.

'Here's a pile of sticks.' She poked about inside the bunker and drew out a handful of chopped wood. 'Where did you put that newspaper we bought to read on the train?' The sticks felt damp, but if the chimney drew well the paper would soon make them catch. She reached over her head automatically and felt along the shelf, and her fingers encountered the box of matches she sought. For all his scholarly ways, Professor Wallace paid scrupulous attention to detail, and it was no surprise to Jo to find he had left a box of matches ready. She struck one. Fortunately these had not gone damp as well, which suggested that the soaking weather streaming against the window panes was of fairly recent origin.

'It's a good job we brought the food with us,' Chris grinned, his spirits restored by the bright flame that set the sticks cracking merrily, and transformed the room into something approaching home. 'The man at the station said he might not be able to bring the rest of our luggage until tomorrow.'

'We can manage until then,' Jo made light of their difficulties. 'Go and find some plates while I unpack the sandwiches.' She gave the boy something to do, it was better than letting him brood. 'I saw a cupboard in the scullery as we came through, there's bound to be some crockery there somewhere.' Laura Wallace had been as thorough as her husband, and there would be utensils available, Jo knew. Chris returned, as she expected him to, with a handful of crocks balanced precariously as he held them up to inspect the pattern.

'They're the odd ones from the kitchen at home.' His voice was wistful, and his sister turned on him with unusual severity.

'You'll have to start calling St Mendoc "home" now, Chris. As soon as the weather lifts, we'll go and explore.' She softened her tone with a promise, and grabbed the kettle as it started to whistle. 'Thank goodness the fire's burned up.' The small room was already beginning to grow warm, and she followed her brother's example and divested herself of her mac. It made a bright splash of colour, hung on a hook behind the door, lending a touch of gaiety to the rather sombre brown of the strictly functional furniture. She would get a couple of comfortable easy chairs as soon as they were settled, she promised herself. Some bright, chintzy curtains and cushions, and the place would look quite different. There were no curtains to the windows now. They were not strictly necessary, since their nearest neighbour was the harbourmaster's house, half a mile away at the foot of the cliff, but pretty curtains would look nice. There was enough money to make the cottage homely. Professors of History were not generally wealthy people, and her father had been no exception; the money that was left would nearly all be swallowed up to provide Chris with a decent education. It would not be fair to take him from his prep school now, when he was showing so much promise, and his headmaster had such high hopes for his future. But she was determined to provide him with a home, to which he could return in the holidays and find her there. A sense of stability was of as much importance as education, and he had lost, in a brutal fashion, the security he had always known until now. Maybe she could find a job locally, enough to bring her in a small income to make things easier. Even, during the season, take in holidaymakers. They could let one room ... Her eyes grew dreamy, making plans, keeping her mind on the future, because it hurt too much to think about the recent past. Even her mac reminded her. Melvin had helped her to choose it.

'Red suits you.' He had put his hands on her shoulders, coming up behind her as she tried on the mac in the shop, and gazing possessively at her reflected figure in the mirror, his eyes meeting hers with that special smile in them that was meant only for her.

Jo had preferred the blue mac she tried on next, but because Melvin liked the red one, she had bought it. It had always been like that with Melvin, she realised now, looking back. She had not noticed it at the time. Like her engagement ring, with the large, rather ornate setting to the stone which she suspected was really more than Melvin could afford, but he liked to boast, to show her off as belonging to him, with the same possessive jealousy that made him resent the friendly advances of her father's students. Chris had not liked her engagement ring very much, either, she remembered.

'Have you lost it?' he asked her, the first time she visited him in hospital, without it being on her finger.

'No.' She hesitated, then decided on the truth. 'I've given it back to Melvin.'

'Have you changed your mind about marrying him?' Academically, Chris took after his father, and his keen mind made him a shrewd observer for his years.

'Yes. I find I don't like him so much as I thought I did.' It was better that Chris did not know the real reason, he had enough problems to face without adding to them.

'I've got the chance of a manager's job in New Zealand,'

Melvin told her jubilantly. 'It's expected the manager will be married, there's a lot of entertaining, apparently.' Melvin loved sophisticated parties, so long as he was the centre of attraction. 'If we got married right away we could go out there together.' It was too soon after her parents' death for her to want to think of getting married, but he was persistent, and so excited about his promotion that Jo forgave him for being insensitive.

'It'll be good for Chris to have a settled home again,' she capitulated, thrusting her own feelings aside. 'The change of scenery might help him to forget the accident.'

'Chris isn't included in my plans,' Melvin rounded on her roughly. 'I don't intend to take on anyone else's kid,' he told her bluntly. 'I don't intend to take on kids of our own, so you might as well get used to the idea.'

She supposed they should have talked about it before they got engaged, but it had not occurred to her. Marriage meant a home—and children. At least, it did to her. She had taken it for granted that it did to Melvin, too. Sadly, after much thought, she gave him back his ring.

'We shall end up by hurting one another. It's better this way.'

He blustered and shouted, as was his habit when he could not get his own way, but when Jo remained quietly determined he flung away in a huff and she did not see him again before she left. Her left hand felt lopsided without his ring, but her heart felt curiously free.

'I think it's stopped raining.' His appetite appeased, Chris limped to the window and looked out. 'The mist's lifted, too. Look, Jo,' he raised his voice excitedly, 'you can see the sea past the end of the garden!'

'Don't go near the cliff edge.' Jo checked his eager move towards the door. 'It doesn't look too safe,' she warned dubiously. 'Stay this side of the fence.' A shaky-looking structure of wire and posts bisected the overgrown patch, several feet away from the actual edge of the cliff, but Jo knew the solid-looking area of turf on the other side might well be only a thin overhang, and the last thing she felt she could face was another accident now.

'You said we could explore,' Chris reminded her hopefully. 'The sun's started to come out.' He raised his face to the thin gleam of sunshine that grew stronger even as he spoke. It was too early in the year to hold much warmth, the earth still lay in that hinterland of winter that Jo knew could turn almost overnight to primrose-decked lanes and mild air, and make a paradise of the bleak cliff with its single tree bent almost double by the searing winds, and still leafless. The sight depressed her. She missed the woods of her home county, and fearful that her own low spirits should affect her brother, she grabbed her wet mac and slipped it on, glad for once of its brazen brightness.

'We'll leave the washing up until we come back. Put your mac on too, the wind will help dry it out.'

'Are you going to take this?' Laughter creased the boy's face as he held out the large door key, and she smiled.

'I'm not facing that struggle again,' she declared. 'I'll slip my purse in my pocket, just in case.' She could not imagine anyone breaking into the cottage set in such a lonely spot, but until her father's solicitor had completed the arrangements for transferring their small capital to the bank at Arlmouth, the nearest town—St Mendoc did not boast a bank of its own—she dared not be careless with the cash she had brought with them. 'I'll bank the fire up before we go.' A warm room would be more welcoming to return to towards evening, she did not want to repeat their chilly entrance into the cottage of a few hours ago. 'Is there something we can put some coal in, ready for tonight? I don't want to have to fumble about in the dark after tea.'

'I saw a big cardboard box in the scullery.' Chris disappeared through the door and returned with a long, flat box.

'It's a fish box.' Jo sniffed cautiously. 'It doesn't smell as if it's been used,' she discovered thankfully.

'It's got a picture of a bird on it, the same as those we saw stacked at the station.' Chris turned it round interestedly, and Jo recognised the graceful print of a tern emblazoned on the side.

'It's a tern—a sea swallow,' she explained. 'D'you remember watching them on the Farne Islands, when we went there two years ago?' The familiar forked tail that gave the sea bird its nickname brought back to her ears the clamour of the breeding ledges, a noise that would soon echo about the grey cottage they had inherited. A brief week or two and the terns would arrive to contest the available nesting sites with the resident birds, doubtless to be followed by the other summer visitors, the human holidaymakers and artists who would temporarily double the population, and add an air of carnival and a welcome extra income to the village community who otherwise relied on the sea for their livelihood.

'There's someone coming.'

Jo straightened up from tugging the garden gate shut, and hastily pulled down her brother's hand.

'Don't point,' she scolded automatically. Then, 'She doesn't look like a visitor . . .'

'I'm not.' The fickle wind that had cleared away the mist from the sea blew Jo's words to the young girl who approached them. She was in her very early teens, Jo judged, but already she showed promise of lovely womanhood, with jet black eyes and hair, familiar colouring along this part of the coast, and telling of ancestry that went back to the early Spanish invaders. She danced rather than walked towards them.

'I'm Melanie,' she announced, and looked at them curiously. 'Melanie Tremayne.' She spoke as if the name ought to mean something to her listeners, but seeing their blank looks she explained, 'I come from the flower farm further along the cliffs towards Arlmouth,' she waved a slim arm along the coastline. 'Tessa told me someone had taken the cottage, so I came along to see,' she said with naïve frankness.

'We were just going to explore.' Chris's tone was noncommittal, and Jo stifled a smile. In another ten years his reaction would not be so indifferent. Responding to the girl's smile, she wondered if the same span of years would destroy the innocence in the huge black eyes. The child possessed unusual beauty, and although she seemed unconscious of it now—she was carelessly dressed in faded jeans and shirt, topped by an old anorak, and shod in incredibly ragged tennis shoes, neither of which boasted a lace—it would not be long before someone, probably a holidaymaker, brought awareness.

'We thought we'd go for a walk to stretch our legs. We've been on the train all the morning.' Jo's friendly tone invited the girl to join them. 'We've never been here before, so we don't know our way about,' she hinted. Despite Chris's lack of interest in the newcomer, Jo wanted him to get to know the local juvenile population, and at least Melanie was a start. She would know the other children in the village, and might provide her brother with an initial introduction.

'I know where the first wild primroses grow.' It was pure, childish boasting, the instinctive challenge from an established member of the herd to a newcomer. 'They're on a ledge in a cleft, half way down the cliff.' She stopped speaking abruptly as Chris stepped out beside Jo. 'There's an easier way down, though.' Her face gentled, seeing his limp. 'And the flowers aren't out yet anyway, it's too early.' She slipped in between the brother and sister and offered her one hand to Jo, her other to Chris, and to Jo's surprise after a brief hesitation he took it. It would be difficult, even for an independent ten-year-old, to resist Melanie's cheerful friendliness.

'Where does that lead to?' Chris pointed, and this time Jo let it ride. He would not forgive her for correcting him in front of the newcomer, and a girl at that.

'That's the path I meant. I like it better than the other one,' their guide said casually. 'When you're sliding on your bottom down the cliff you can't look round. You get some lovely views from this one.' Jo warmed to her kindly tact, and even the boy responded.

'Does it come out on the beach?'

'It drops down by the side of Penderick Creek. You can see Penderick House from the top of this slope.' Melanie considerately slowed her steps as the cliff rose towards a sharp point not far ahead, and chatted on amiably. 'You can't see the house from by the creek itself, the woods are too thick.'

'Woods?' Jo's heart lifted.

'Mmm, they're lovely in the spring. They're private, of course.' The girl's gay laugh, and the way she tossed her head, making her heavy raven mane swing across her slender shoulders, told Jo that she made light of the prohibitions of ownership.

'I'd like to explore them.' The ghost of a grin lit Chris's eyes, and Jo frowned at him.

'Don't go trespassing, and get into trouble,' she warned him, but just the same she felt glad to see something of his old daredevil spirit show itself again.

'We won't,' Melanie promised, and oddly Jo felt as if the child had taken herself and Chris under her wing. Also, that she could be trusted. 'Look, there's Penderick House.' She pointed to a squat grey stone house lying almost directly below them, on what looked like a small peninsula. It was flanked on three sides by a thick belt of trees, sheltering the house on its seaward side. On the fourth, extensive gardens sloped down to the shiny waters of the creek that ran like a silver ribbon past the dark, silent trees rising above it. Smoke curled from several of the chimneys, and for some reason Jo felt surprised.

'I thought it might be a National Trust property,' she hazarded. In size it resembled the manor houses she was familiar with at home. 'Open to the public in the summer months—that sort of thing?'

'Oh no, the Pendericks live there themselves,' Melanie put her right, casually. 'They're the fishing family. The ones with the pictures of the tern on their boxes.'

For a fishing family they lived in a palatial home, Jo thought drily, but she said nothing.

'We've got one of their boxes in our cottage,' Chris remembered. 'Jo knew it was a tern—she told me.' He did a bit of boasting of his own. 'Something like him—I think?' he eyed a wailing gull that floated overhead.

'That's only an old gull,' the girl's voice was scornful. 'The terns have got forked tails, and they don't come until about April, the same as the land swallows. There's another month to go yet. When they come I'll show you where their breeding ledges are if you like,' she offered.

'Show us now,' Chris begged eagerly, his scorn of girls forgotten.

'I can't,' Melanie refused. 'Tessa said I'd got to be back before tea. She'll be mad with me if I'm late, I skipped helping with the washing up at lunch time,' she grinned unrepentantly.

'Tessa?' Melanie did not seem the type who would call her mother by her Christian name.

'My sister. She keeps house for my father. She says I can take over when I'm older and give her a chance to get married,' Melanie threw the information at them carelessly.

'I'll come with you as far as the creek, then I'll have to go back.' She dug her heels in with a practised braking action that Chris and Jo copied as the downward slope got steeper, and their knees ached with the strain of holding them back.

'Phew, that was tough going,' Chris admitted, and Jo looked at him sharply.

'Are you tired?'

'No, I can make it.' His chin came up in the familiar gesture.

'The path's almost flat from here,' Melanie assured Jo. 'It's the most interesting part of the walk,' she stopped Chris's protest that he could climb the cliff back again easily enough. 'There's a lot of wild life along the creek, if you're interested. The path forks not far from here, take the left-hand path and you'll come out near the village. You'll know your way back from there.'

With a gay wave, and a promise, 'I'll come again as soon as I can,' she left them, skipping from rock to rock along the shore like a gay sea sprite, then she rounded the cliff and was gone, leaving Jo and Chris feeling curiously alone.

'These flaky bits of stone make smashing skimmers.' With young enthusiasm Chris picked up the nearest and skimmed it across the water. 'It bounced three times,' he counted delightedly. 'I'll try another—oh, look, here's a bit that's striped with red. Would it be any good for you to make a ring or bracelet with?' He took a keen interest in Jo's hobby of making jewellery, and was her chief source of supply of stones in odd shapes or colours when her clerical work for her father precluded her from searching for her own. She would have plenty of time to do that for herself, now.

'It's pretty.' Jo took it from him and examined it. 'This looks like a good place to find stones.'

'You could start up a business,' Chris suggested jokingly. 'Handmade jewellery for the holidaymakers.'

'It's an idea,' Jo realised. 'It's worth thinking about, anyway. Now, which fork did Melanie say we'd got to take?' Immersed in their talk, they had reached the Y end of the path without realising it.

'The left—no, the right ... I've forgotten,' Chris admitted guiltily. 'She said the path was flat from now on ...'

'It'll be the right-hand one, then,' Jo chose the flattest-looking of the two.

'It looks sort of private ...' Chris voiced his doubts a hundred yards further on, as banks of rhododendrons took the place of the rough scrub running almost to the edge of the creek, and a sudden blaze of yellow proclaimed the presence of a sheet of daffodils, naturalised under the trees in disorderly clumps so that, looking uphill, they made a carpet of living gold.

'Shhh! Look in the water. Oh, we've disturbed him ...' A heron stood statuesque in the shallows at the side of the creek, and as they rounded a clump of evergreens it took to its wings, their slow languid-seeming beat taking it with deceptive speed across to the other side of the water, and out of sight.

'What the blazes do you mean by barging up the path like that, and frightening my heron away?'

A man rose from concealment on the other side of the rhododendron clump and regarded them with a furious blue glare. Black brows met in an angry line over a strong nose, and his deeply tanned face, topped by hair as dark as Melanie's, was tightly hostile. 'Can't you see this is private property?' he fumed. 'You're trespassing!'

He stood foursquare in their path, denying them further progress, and Jo halted, nonplussed, with Chris behind her. Melanie must have told them the left-hand path after all. They had taken the wrong one, and obviously wandered into the grounds of Penderick House. This must be one of the Penderick family confronting them. Jo regarded the six-foot-plus of angry householder, and decided she could well do without the acquaintance of this particular new neighbour. She much preferred Melanie.

'I'm extremely sorry,' she apologised immediately, trying to appease his wrath. 'I didn't mean to disturb your bird-watching.' It seemed a small matter for the man to get so worked up about, she thought. Living at Penderick House, he must have loads of opportunities to watch the herons in the creek.

'Melanie told us which path to take, but we forgot,' Chris added his own apology, and loyally backed up his sister.

'Then you'll know in future to take the left-hand fork of the path,' the man retorted coldly.

'I've said I'm sorry,' Jo sparked, stung into anger herself by his curt response to the child. 'It was a pure mistake.'

'Then kindly don't repeat it.' He was in no way appeased. 'It might be months before a heron stands in that particular position again, with the light as it is now. You've ruined my work!' He waved a sketching block at her, and Jo caught a glimpse of a half finished drawing of the bird they had just disturbed. From her brief sighting she could see it was beautifully executed, but obviously incomplete. 'It's been a complete waste of time,' the man snapped, and confirmed her dismayed realisation that not only had she disrupted the heron's peaceful search for food, but in so doing had put the artist's model to flight—and irretrievably enraged the artist.

CHAPTER TWO

'I CAN'T do more than apologise,' Jo said stiffly. 'Come on, Chris, we'll go back.' She turned her back on the angry blue eyes, that had the crowsfeet creases of a sailor used to squinting against dazzle on the water, and that seemed to bore right through her rather than just look at her.

'It's a long way back to the fork,' Chris complained. 'My leg aches from coming down the slope of that cliff.'

His limp was more pronounced as he turned away, as it always was when he became tired, and Jo looked at him worriedly.

'Wait a minute. There's no need to go right back to the fork.'

Jo turned back and stared in surprise. Was it really the dark-visaged stranger who had called to her? She looked beyond him, half expecting to see someone else there, but there was no one in sight.

'We wouldn't dream of trespassing any further.' Her chin came up in the same gesture that Chris used, and her voice was cold. 'I can find the way back perfectly well,' she assured him. He need not fear she would get lost and trespass on his property again.

'I don't doubt it.' Anger still glinted in the blue eyes that fixed her with a compelling gimlet stare. 'I'm thinking of the boy, not of you,' their owner told her bluntly. 'There's a bridge across the creek from our side on to the public footpath on the other bank. It'll save you over a mile of walking. If you'll allow me to show you,' as she still hesitated he gave her a mock bow and gestured with his arm along the path, at the same time stepping to one side so that she could

20

proceed past him. Automatically, Jo found herself obeying him, as he had intended her to, she thought with a quick flash of resentment. But there was Chris to consider, and she swallowed her pride and walked past the artist with her chin held high. Despite the surgeon's instructions to let her brother use his leg normally—'give it exercise and eventually the limp will disappear'—she did not want to try this new-found strength too far.

'There's the bridge.' A hand as brown tanned as his face drew her eyes along the length of the creek. 'You can see the parapet where the creek bends.'

He doesn't think it's necessary to see us off the premises, Jo thought with an inward flash of amusement. Perhaps it's beneath his dignity . . .

'I'll come with you as far as the bridge steps,' he disabused her. 'It's useless me staying here, the heron won't come back today,' he said regretfully, but his tone was milder.

I hope Chris doesn't notice, Jo worried, realising that the stranger's consideration sprang from compassion, which was to his credit, but might hurt the boy's pride.

'D'you think he'll come back tomorrow? The heron, I mean?' Jo heaved a sigh of relief. Chris's eager question held nothing but interest. 'It's a shame to frighten him away. Dad took us birdwatching to the Farne Islands the year before last,' he added conversationally.

'So you've been birdwatching before?'

She could not be sure whether he was being sarcastic or not. His face was expressionless, giving nothing away. But even he must realise that other people besides himself might be interested in the same hobby, she thought waspishly.

'We're members of the National Trust,' she told him curtly. 'We thought this might belong to them as well.' She nodded towards the low stone house, framed from this angle by the daffodils, and at this nearer distance revealing itself as old, but remarkably well preserved, and much larger even than it had looked from the cliff. Certainly a property that for historical as well as aesthetic reasons might merit the attention of the Trust if its owner should ever decide to sell.

Her remark was spurred by an urge to deflate the present occupier, but to her annoyance it seemed to have the opposite effect. Some of the angry indifference disappeared from his expression, and his face showed cautious interest.

'I'm a member too. The Trust has got quite a lot of land along the cliffs not far from here.'

'I wish I could draw like you,' Chris interrupted her disinterested, 'I know...' and she lapsed into thankful silence. Whatever she said seemed to annoy the stranger, though she forgave the child's apparent friendliness; Chris had had one or two as yet unsuccessful forays into the world of art, which seemed to have heightened rather than detracted from his enthusiasm. He eyed the half-completed sketch in the man's hand with frank envy. 'I've tried sketching birds, but they won't stay still for long enough,' he complained, and surprised a laugh out of his listener.

'We all have the same trouble,' he confessed with a twinkle, that made his face look quite different, almost friendly, if that were possible. 'And when I do get a bird to stand still for a few minutes, someone comes along and frightens it away.' He looked straight at Jo as he spoke, and the ire was back in his voice.

'We didn't mean...' she began indignantly.

'Dan!' A man's voice hallooed from the top of the slope by the house, and a figure waved wildly to attract their companion's attention. 'Dan! The phone—for you,' he shouted.

'Oh——!' The man called Dan growled under his

breath, and Jo smothered a laugh with difficulty. It was evidently not his day.

'Coming!' he called back, and reaching out grasped Jo's arm in a grip that he might not have meant to be hard, but nevertheless made her wince. 'Take the steps across the bridge,' he instructed, pointing with his other hand, 'then turn right along the footpath on the other bank. Do you think you'll remember, this time?' he turned to Chris, and his lips lifted slightly at the boy's emphatic nod. 'In that case, about half a mile you should come to the lane that leads straight back to the village.'

'We know our way from there, thank you,' Jo answered him primly, rescuing her arm, but determinedly refusing to rub it although it tingled from the strength of his fingers. 'Come along, Chris.' She gave him a cool nod, and was disconcerted to find his keen gaze on her face.

'I...' he began.

'Dan! The phone!' The figure by the house waxed impatient.

'Oh, all right, I'm coming!' the man called Dan shouted back irritably, and without a second look in their direction he turned abruptly on his heel and strode uphill through the daffodils as swiftly as if he was crossing level ground.

'That'd be Dan Penderick,' Melanie informed them when told of their adventure. 'He's the middle one. Julian's the eldest, and Lance is the last.'

'Three of them?' Jo's eyebrows rose. If the other two Pendericks were as short-tempered as Dan, it must be a scratchy household! 'Do they all fish for a living?' she enquired. She was not really interested, but Melanie seemed to have taken over the role of guide and mentor to the newcomers and enjoyed passing on her local information to them. Also, since they had come to live at St Mendoc, they would have to learn about the community sooner or later, and the young girl seemed to know all about everybody. Probably by now the occupants of St Mendoc knew all about herself and Chris, she realised ruefully, or at least as much as Melanie had gathered from her time with them.

'Julian doesn't fish, he's not strong enough. He looks after the canning factory instead,' the girl enlarged. 'Dan Penderick looks after the fleet.'

'The fleet?' Jo looked up interestly. Melanie had earlier described the Pendericks as 'the fishing family', an odd label in a community that were nearly all fishermen, and one that did not seem in accord with the Penderick style of living.

'They run a fleet of inshore boats.' Melanie accepted her glass of lemonade and a piece of gingerbread, and settled on the hearthrug beside Chris. 'They keep their own canning factory going, and sell their surplus catch at the open auction. The boats anchor up in the harbour on the other side of Penderick Head, where the village street peters out,' she described the location with graphic accuracy.

'Penderick House. Penderick Creek. Penderick Head. It all seems to be Pendericks around here,' Jo grumbled.

'It is mostly, I suppose.' Melanie accepted the local pecking order calmly. 'Lance doesn't skipper his own boat yet, though,' she added. 'My father says he wants to, but Dan won't let him. He says he's too young, and too irresponsible.' She spoke with the sympathy of fellow feeling, and Jo smiled. Melanie had probably had the same sobriquet applied to herself often enough to be used to it.

'Can't he ask—who did you say the eldest one was? Julian?' It amused her to think someone might stand up to Dan Penderick, his autocratic manner when they met still nettled her.

'Julian Penderick wouldn't interfere,' her informant said wisely. 'He's the quiet one—gentle,' she added. 'He got something or other when he was little, and it left him frail.'

She wrinkled her face, trying to remember what it was. 'It's the same as that mint sweet you get in a tube.'

'You mean polio? Infantile paralysis?' Light dawn on Jo.

'That's right.' Now her description was satisfactorily completed Melanie lost interest in things that were mere history to her. 'Are you really going to turn this into a necklace?' She fingered the red striped stone that Chris showed her with an impressed expression.

'I thought it would make a nice pendant,' Jo responded. 'I've got a claw setting and a chain somewhere. If you like I'll polish and set it, and you can have it to keep,' she offered generously. It would be a small thank-you to the child for befriending them, she thought. They had seen no one else to speak to since they arrived. Except Dan Penderick, of course, but that was a meeting they could well have done without. She dismissed Dan Penderick from her mind.

He intruded once or twice between herself and her work as she sat polishing the piece of striped stone beside the fire several days later, his dark, angry face outlined by a fringe of daffodils.

'I do wish this rain would stop.' For some reason Dan Penderick's persistent intrusion on her peaceful occupation made her irritable. As her intrusion had made him, she realised honestly, but the thought did not make her any less cross.

'Melanie says it's rained on and off for six days and nights,' Chris offered, his interest more on the book of birds he was studying than on what his sister was saying. 'They had a lot of frosty weather before that. She says it's unusual to have bad frosts down here.'

Warm winters would mean smaller fuel bills, Jo thought thankfully. That would be a help in their present circumstances. And if she took in one or two visitors during the summer months, she might accumulate enough capital to make a reasonable stock of jewellery during the winter.

Chris's suggestion had taken root, and the more she thought about it the more attractive it seemed. She would need an occupation, alone in the cottage during the winter, with Chris away at school. She wondered what age Melanie's sister was. It would be nice if they could be friends.

Thinking more hopefully about the future, she fell asleep that night only to find she still could not shut Dan Penderick out of her mind. He strode through her dreams in the same arrogant manner that he had blocked her path along the side of the creek, his piercing blue eyes watching her as she struggled along the shore against the wind, looking in vain for striped stones to make a bracelet to match Melanie's pendant. The girl's gay laugh rang out over the blustery gusts. 'It's private, of course,' she kept saying, and Jo knew she was trespassing again, but this time there was no other path to lead her away from Dan Penderick, and whether she wanted to or not she had to go on, to face his anger, and his booming voice that rose above the crash of the waves as he bade her sternly to turn round and go back to where the path forked. She stumbled and fell, and the waves crashed louder, drowning even the rumble of his voice.

'I can't find the path.' She sat up and shouted, trying to make him hear. Trying to make him understand. The sound of her own voice woke her up.

'Jo?' Her bedroom light snapped on, and turned her sleep daze into wide-awake reality.

'Chris, what are you doing at this time of night? What's the matter?' She was out of bed in a flash, the months of emergency just behind her still speeding her reactions where her brother was concerned.

'Nothing's the matter. At least, not with me.' He climbed on to the side of her bed, and curled his bare feet under the blankets for warmth.

'Then what are you doing out of bed?' she scolded. Her

immediate panic gone, she automatically pulled his dressing gown closer round him and tied the cord. 'Your feet are frozen!'

'There was a loud rumbling noise, and then a crash. There it goes again.' His hand sought Jo's and gripped her tight.

'It must be an explosion somewhere.' She raised startled eyes to the ceiling, which for a second seemed to rock above them. The lamp hung from the centre gyrated crazily, then as the ominous rumbling died down it steadied again, and Jo's heartbeat began to swing back to normal with it.

'The crash I heard sounded like crockery,' Chris found his voice as the noise subsided. 'It came from the direction of the scullery, anyway.' Now Jo was awake and in charge his fright turned to excited interest. 'There was a tinkling sound after the crash.'

'Let's go and see.' The noise stopped and the ceiling lamp returned to normal except for a slight pendulum movement that grew less even as she watched it. 'It must have been the first rumble that roused me. I was dreaming, and thought it was the waves on the beach.' She chatted on cheerfully, as much for her own sake as for the boy's. At this hour—she glanced at the clock, and the hands showed half past two—the cottage seemed even more isolated than it did in the daytime. 'Oh, my goodness, what a mess!' She flicked the light on in the kitchen and surveyed the row of hooks on the kitchen dresser, that now supported a row of brightly coloured crock cup handles—and no cups. Her dismayed glance took in the shards of their precious crockery, scattered all over the floor.

'There were four mugs left inside the cupboard.' Ever an optimist, Chris sought what had been saved rather than what had been destroyed. 'They're still in one piece—look,' he opened the cupboard door and revealed the four mugs, jumbled now among the other things by the rocking of the cupboard, but still triumphantly intact.

'Perhaps it's a nuclear submarine or something,' Chris said hopefully. His reading matter included the usual ten-year-old's adventure series in the weekly comics, and his vivid imagination did the rest.

'And perhaps there's a quarry somewhere nearby, and they've chosen now to dynamite a fresh supply of stone,' Jo said more practically. 'All the houses round here seem to be built with the same grey material, even Penderick House.' It gave her an odd satisfaction that Penderick House should in this respect be no different from their own humble abode. 'I expect it's a local stone, and the quarry isn't too far away. It can't be, for their dynamite to shake the cottage like that.' She hoped they would not blast the stone too often; apart from crockery being expensive it would probably crack the ceilings. It might even have cracked the window panes as it was. She would have to look in the morning.

'Surely they wouldn't use dynamite half way through the night?' Chris sounded puzzled. 'If it's shaken our house like this, it's probably woken up half the village.'

'They might have to use it during the night hours to save disrupting traffic or something,' Jo hazarded a guess. 'And if the village has been woken up, they'll probably be used to it and go right back to sleep again. The same as you must,' she forestalled further flights of fancy. 'Oh, very well, if you're hungry,' she intercepted his hopeful glance at the cake tin, 'get two of those mugs and we'll take a drink and a piece of gingerbread each back to bed with us.' She herded him firmly back to his own room. 'We'll clear up this mess in the morning.'

'Did Chris shout Boo! behind you when you were drying up, or something?' Melanie poked a laughing face round the door as Jo dealt with the broken crockery the next morning.

'Golly, what a mess!' She sounded awestruck.

'It is, and he didn't,' Jo commented in reverse order. 'And you'll have to have your elevenses from a mug, there isn't a whole cup in the house,' she told their visitor ruefully. 'That explosion last night broke the lot.' She indicated the cupless handles, still dangling uselessly from the hooks.

'What explosion?' Melanie's eyes widened, and she perched on the table, all ears. 'I didn't hear any explosion. What happened?'

'You didn't hear it?' Jo looked at her incredulously. 'You must sleep like a log,' she said enviously. 'Swing your feet up a bit while I brush under you.'

'I haven't come to be in the way.' Melanie jumped lightly to the floor. 'I've come to fetch Chris. I thought we'd go and see if that heron had come back—that is, if it's all right with you?' She remembered her manners.

'You're not to trespass.' Jo spoke firmly. 'I won't have Chris getting into any more trouble with Dan Penderick. Once was quite enough,' she said feelingly.

'We'll keep to the public footpath. Honestly.' Huge black eyes gazed seriously into Jo's, then lightened with a twinkle. 'I promise we won't trespass until Chris can run fast enough not to get caught,' she laughed gaily, encouraged by Chris's mischievous chuckle from by the door.

'See that you don't,' Jo threatened, hiding her own amusement with difficulty. 'At least that'll give me a week or two to establish reasonable relations with my neighbours before you two can do any damage.' She could not scold when Chris was already so much stronger. His excursions about the cliffs and beach with Melanie had tanned his white face, and the resultant appetite had filled out his thin body, and already his limp was less noticeable than when they arrived. She had the girl to thank for this, and realisation made her remember the pendant.

'Put it on to see if you like it,' she suggested, and Melanie's face lit up.

'Isn't it pretty?' She fingered the stone, polished now to a smooth shine that brought out the colour, and held by three silver claws at the end of a long chain.

'I wish I'd got a box to put it in,' Jo said regretfully, 'but my things are still with my luggage. And that's still at the station.' Brisk efficiency did not seem an attribute of the local travel facilities, the population of St Mendoc had inherited the easygoing *'mañana'* of their Spanish forebears.

'I've got a big shell I can keep it in when I'm not wearing it. But I want to wear it now.' Melanie danced off to show her treasure to Chris, and Jo called after them:

'Be back by one o'clock for lunch!' Hunger would probably drive them back a lot earlier, she thought with a smile, and set about preparing vegetables for three in case the girl should decide to stay and eat with them. She was half way through making a bread and butter pudding when the rumbling they had heard in the night started again. It was hardly noticeable at first, and she spread butter and jam with a liberal hand, intent on catering for a couple of ravenous appetites, when a series of thuds arrested her knife in mid-air. For some unexplained reason her heart began to hammer wildly, and her mouth felt dry. Two thuds—a third—then a sort of slithering rush that died into a silence that seemed as ominous as the noise. Jo stood stock still in the tiny kitchen, frozen into immobility while she waited for she knew not what. There had been no explosion, only the rumble. And that had seemed to come, not from a distance, as the shock waves of rock blasting would travel, but from right under her feet, through the very foundations of the cliff itself. It could not be water surge in a cave under them, the tide was well out—she could see a wide strip of dun-coloured beach over the edge of the cliff beyond the back garden.

The rumble came again, louder this time, and the utensils on the kitchen table danced an accompaniment. The noise increased, filling the house, drowning her gasp of terror, and her ability to think, let alone to act. The floor rocked wildly under her feet, and as she watched, petrified with fear, a large crack appeared and zigzagged lightning fashion diagonally across the outside kitchen wall.

'Jo! Jo Wallace!'

Running footsteps pounded up the front path, and a man's voice roared her name, demanding—commanding—that she answer.

'Jo, where are you? Answer me!' The front door crashed open, and banged shut again with the force of its rebound off the wall. 'Jo!'

Jo shivered. The shout was almost as terrifying as the rumble. Her hands flew to her mouth, and the knife dropped from her nerveless fingers and fell with a clatter on to the floor.

'There you are. Why didn't you answer me?' Dan Penderick stood framed in the doorway, guided by the clatter of the knife. He had to stoop almost double to get his head under the lintel, and in two strides he was across the room and gripping Jo by the wrist. His fingers closed with crushing force about her slender bones, and she drew back with an involuntary cry.

'Don't be a fool,' he told her roughly. 'I haven't come here to hurt you. Can't you see the place is about to fall down round your ears any minute now?' he cried.

The rumbling started again as he spoke, and with a loud bang the mortar between the bricks gave way, and the crack in the kitchen wall widened and light shone through.

'Come on, out!' Without ceremony Dan pulled her after him towards the outer door. She rounded the table in a headlong rush, propelled by his grip on her wrist, and stepped on the fallen knife. It twisted under her sandal and she stumbled and went to her knees. Terror-struck, she looked up and saw the man's mouth move, but what he shouted was drowned in a searing crescendo of noise as a large corner of the ceiling gave way and collapsed on to the spot where she had stood seconds before. The next moment it was blotted from her sight as he stooped over her. With no more effort than if she had been a baby he scooped her into his arms and pressed her face against his rough blue fisherman's jersey. Crouching low, so that his body protected her from falling debris, he spun round and ran for the front door. With scarcely a pause he raised his foot and kicked at the closed wood, and Jo heard it splinter under the force of the attack, heard the accelerated screech of the hinges as it slammed open and let them through, and then they were out into the open air, and running up the garden path.

Her rescuer treated the garden gate with the same scant ceremony which he had accorded the cottage door, as he ran hard, away from the cottage, away from the cliff edge, and the tearing, roaring sound that bore into Jo's consciousness what it was that the noise in the night had foretold. And gave her, too, the despairing knowledge that for the second time in as many months, she and Chris had lost their home.

After what seemed an age the man stopped running. He slowed and came to a halt, and Jo felt his arm leave the back of her head where it had kept her face pressed hard against him, and she looked up and blinked. Gently he set her on her feet, but he still kept both his arms about her, holding her close against him as if he was afraid she might not be able to stand. It was a wise precaution. She trembled from head to foot, shaking as if with ague at the realisation of what might have been, and, thanks to Dan Penderick, was not.

She felt him lean back against something, drawing her with him, and became conscious of his hard breathing, and the strong, swift beat of his heart through his blue jersey, reacting to his urgent flight with her extra weight as a burden. Slowly his heartbeat steadied. Her ear came to just the height where he pressed her against him, and as it calmed to a normal steady thud through the blue jersey, so her trembling lessened, her courage renewed by the strength of the man who held her. She raised her head and looked round, and saw they were leaning against the bonnet of a Land-Rover pickup. She glanced at the cottage. It leaned drunkenly towards the edge of the cliff—a new edge, that now came almost up to the back door. The overhang of cliff, and the entire back garden, had disappeared in a tremendous rock fall. If she and Chris ... She shuddered and closed her eyes, and felt her rescuer tighten his arms round her reassuringly.

'Chris?' She opened her eyes again, wide with terror. 'Chris and Melanie—they said they might go and look for stones on the way to the creek.' Feebly she struggled against his grasp, and her efforts to free herself became frantic as his hold on her remained firm. 'They might be...' She choked, unable to go on, and of a sudden her eyes became blurred with tears.

'Chris and Melanie are safe at Penderick House. I left them with Julian—my brother,' he explained. 'They're quite safe.' He emphasised his words with a slight shake, and she gulped and drew her hand hastily across her eyes. Although he had undoubtedly saved her life, pride forbade her to cry in front of Dan Penderick.

'Then how——?' She raised her eyes to his face. They glistened with the tears she refused to let fall, the colour of beech bark after rain, and his face tightened with a peculiar expression that made him pause for a while before he answered her question.

'How did I come to be here?' His voice was low and oddly soft, so different from the last time she heard him speak that it might have been someone else talking. Even through her daze of shock, she was conscious of the difference. 'Chris and Melanie came along the creek to see if the heron had come back. Oh, don't worry,' his lips tilted suddenly, 'they kept to the public footpath until I invited them both over on to our side. Melanie showed me the pendant you gave her. It was beautifully done,' he complimented Jo, talking her shock away, feeling her relax slowly in his arms at the reassuring sound of a human voice. A strong voice, that sounded as if it could cope with any emergency, even a rock fall. 'Then young Melanie,' he spoke as if he knew her well; he probably knew the whole family, in such a small community as St Mendoc no one could remain a stranger for long, 'young Melanie asked me if I heard the explosion last night. She was full of it, and when Julian and I questioned her Chris supplied the details that she left out. When they said you were still at the cottage, I didn't waste any time,' he said grimly. 'Didn't you realise what was going on?' A touch of impatience tinged his voice now he saw that she was in a fit state to listen to him. 'If that lot had collapsed last night, you and your brother might have been killed. As it was...' He stopped abruptly, his lips tightening.

'Do you think I don't realise that?' Jo stiffened away from him, and cautiously he lowered his arms, keeping one still loosely about her waist, but not holding her against him any more. 'But how was I to know the cliff would collapse? I didn't realise what the rumbling meant, I thought it was an explosion in a quarry or something. The cliffs must have stood like that for hundreds of years,' she protested.

'Probably thousands.' The dry tone was more nearly like the Dan Penderick of her first acquaintance. 'But remember the freak weather conditions we've had since last year,' he pointed out. 'There was that hot dry summer, that lasted for months on end. Then frosts such as this area knows only once in a century or so. After that, for good measure we had prolonged rain, then more frosts, now rain again. The rock soaked up the water like a sponge after the drought, the frost expanded and flaked it, and now the edges have crumbled. There've been a lot of falls among the cliffs right along the coast, but nothing,' his eyes took in the wreckage in front of them, 'nothing so serious as this one up to now.'

'That's news to me,' Jo answered tartly. 'We've been living in the Thames Valley until now.'

'But you . . .'

'We experienced the same weather,' she conceded, 'but I was not to know what local effect it might have.' She stoutly defended her ignorance. 'My father wouldn't have bought the cottage if he thought it might be unsafe,' she pointed out.

'If I'd thought it was unsafe, I wouldn't have sold it to him,' her companion answered quietly, and Jo stared at him.

'I didn't know it belonged to you?'

'It did. And thank goodness I transferred the insurance to your father's name,' he said seriously. 'At least you won't have to suffer a financial loss.'

'I'll have to get lodgings of some sort.' Slowly she stirred and stood independently, her mind beginning to work again. 'There'll probably be somewhere in the village we can get rooms until I've had time to think what to do.' It was imperative to get a roof over their heads, if only for a few nights, to give her time to sort things out. 'This insurance?' She grasped at his words. 'I'll have to ask our solicitor. My father——' she stopped.

'I know.' Dan Penderick watched her struggle for composure, and nodded his approval of her success. 'Chris apparently confided in Melanie, and she told me.' Considerately he looked away from her then, out to sea with the screwed up squint against the strong light that beat back from the water. Still without looking at her, he went on, 'You'll stay with us for the moment, of course. Since the cottage originally belonged to me I feel responsible,' he insisted, firmly stilling her vehement protest. 'Hannah will look after you. You look as if you need it,' he told her curtly, his eyes taking in her slight figure as if he saw her for the first time, and the fine bone structure that showed too plainly through her cheeks. 'Give yourself a few days, if only for the boy's sake,' he urged. 'We're not all ogres at Penderick House.' His lips lifted again, and Jo flushed. The last place she wanted to be was under the same roof as Dan Penderick. He was the last person she wanted to be under an obligation to, either, and now she owed him her life.

'While you're with us, Julian can sort out the insurance for you,' he persisted, seeing her reluctance. 'He's the business head of the family, and Chris has already made friends with him.' He deliberately drove her into a corner, using Chris as a lever for the second time, so that once again she would obey him.

'I'll have to think ... I must get my mac and my purse, it's in the pocket, hung on the living room door,' she digressed, bidding for time, and took a few tentative steps towards the cottage. It was all the ready money she had, and she had no intention of accepting charity for herself or Chris. 'I'll go and get it now the fall has stopped.'

'You'll do no such thing!' Her companion gripped her wrist again, angrily this time. 'You'll be mad to try and go into that place again. If another rock fall starts, the whole house would go. I forbid you to try,' he said sternly.

'You can't forbid me to do anything!' Jo rounded on him. She knew she was being unreasonable, that he was talking sound good sense, but accumulated shock and a return of Dan Penderick's autocratic manner were more than her nerves could bear. Her eyes sparkled with anger and she tried futilely to twist her wrist from his grip.

'I—oh!' To her dismay the jersey-clad figure that held her began to sway as if he stood on the deck of one of his inshore fishing boats in a bad storm, and Jo put her hand to her head dizzily.

'I forbid you to faint until we reach Hannah!' A hint of alarm sounded in his stern tone. 'She'll know how to look after you.' Implying that he did not? He seemed intent on taking herself and Chris under his wing, whether she wanted it or not. Or perhaps he merely meant to hand them over to the ubiquitous Hannah, whoever she might be, and then wash his hands of them both. His voice came from a long distance away, booming in her ears as it had boomed through her dreams the night before, and desperately she fought to hold on to her failing senses. Hazily she felt his arms go round her for the second time that morning as once again he scooped her up, and this time deposited her on to the front seat of the Land-Rover. She felt him fiddle with the seat belt, adjusting it round her so that she would not slip if she became unconscious and then the engine broke into purring life, carrying her, she realised dimly, back to Penderick House—exactly as its owner intended.

CHAPTER THREE

'My, but you had a lucky escape!'

Jo opened her eyes and found a plump, motherly woman with greying hair looking down at her. She looked to be in her early fifties, and her apple-cheeked face was full of concern.

'Where...?' Jo struggled to a sitting position and found she was tucked up in somebody's bed. Memory came flooding back and answered her question for her. She altered it. 'Where's Chris?'

'He's with Mr Julian.' A beam lit her companion's homely face. 'Those two seem to be getting along fine. He's a bright little lad, isn't he?' She evidently liked children, thought Jo with relief.

'You must be Hannah?' she hazarded. The way she had said 'Mr Julian' marked her as not being an actual member of the family.

'That's right, I'm Hannah,' the kindly face beamed with the self-confidence of a privileged member of the household, albeit not one of the Pendericks. 'Mr Dan had you put in this room because it's got the small one leading off it. The little lad can sleep in there, and he'll feel you're close by if he finds a strange house offputting. It's the old nursery,' her informant explained.

'It's a lovely room,' Jo said slowly, looking about her. Appreciatively, because she liked old furniture, and rugs scattered about a floor of oak as thick as ship's timbers, making soft splashes of colour against the dark wood that offered the skill of the weavers of the world for the delight of the occupant of the room, and betrayed the Pendericks—

38

or at least their ancestors—as having fished the universe for
their treasures, which Jo's not untutored glance told her
were probably priceless.

'I don't remember coming to bed?'

'You don't need to try,' Hannah told her firmly. 'It was
before lunch when Mr Dan brought you home, and now it's
almost five o'clock. We're having dinner at six tonight because of the tide, and you must be hungry,' she said briskly.
She did not explain what the tide had to do with dinner,
but Jo had enough puzzles on her mind without trying to
sort out this one.

'I remember having something to drink.'

'Mr Julian gave you a glass of brandy. You were that
white when Mr Dan brought you in.'

'I can still taste it.' Jo wrinkled her face with disgust.
She remembered a man—a tall, thin man, with a stoop and
a fair beard, and a wonderfully gentle voice—bending over
her and pressing a glass to her lips. So that was Julian, the
elder brother. From her hazy recollection he seemed not at
all like Dan. Gentle, Melanie had called him, and he
soothed her as tenderly as a woman when the potent drink
he coaxed down her broke the last barriers of her self-
control, and she wept. Shame flushed her cheeks as she remembered her tears, that she had refused to let fall in front
of Dan. Or in front of Melvin, for that matter. She had not
cried since her parents were killed, a numb sense of shock
carrying her through the dreadful weeks that followed;
even through her subsequent broken engagement. Her need
to provide Chris with a firm anchor and a new home had
bolstered her own courage until now, and it had finally
broken on an unexpected kindness. Vaguely, she remembered someone talking to her; it must have been Julian
because she felt his beard tickle her forehead, but she could
not remember what it was he said. And then, as exhaustion
staunched the flow of tears, she heard another, stronger

voice—Dan's voice—say, 'I'll take her up to Hannah.'

She felt herself raised in strong arms and lifted up, but she was beyond resisting, beyond even voicing a protest. Wearily she rested her wet cheek against his dark blue fisherman's jersey and thankfully allowed herself to be enveloped in the warm mantle of blackness that descended on her consciousness, and gave her merciful oblivion.

'I *am* hungry,' she realised, surprised into full wakefulness. 'My clothes . . .?' It dawned on her that she was in a nightdress. Investigation revealed it as one of her own.

'Your dress and sandals were all dust and plaster,' Hannah told her, 'but it doesn't matter. Mr Dan fetched your luggage from the station for you.' She moved aside so that Jo could see her cases piled on top of a long, low sea chest, complete even to the iron bands, that rested under one window. 'You've plenty of time to have a bath and change before the gong goes, your bathroom's through that door in the corner.'

'I'll have to collect Chris.'

'Don't worry, I've tubbed him for you,' smiled her companion. 'He told me all about the last few months.' Her face sobered, and the glance she gave Jo was filled with compassion. 'You've had a real bad time,' she sympathised. 'You'll be able to rest up and have a break, now you're here.'

'I shan't be staying,' Jo answered. 'Oh, perhaps for a night or two.' Not more than one night, if I can help it, she added silently to herself. It was one thing to accept Dan Penderick's hospitality when she had no option, but that did not give him the right to decide her destiny for her. 'I'll get rooms in the village until I've decided what to do about the cottage,' she continued as Hannah still lingered. 'What shall I wear to go down to dinner?' She hesitated, and sought the other woman's help. 'My evening clothes will probably need hanging up for an hour or two to let the rumples out. They've been in the cases for nearly a week now.'

'We don't dress for dinner in the week, miss,' Hannah assured her. 'Only at weekeneds. An ordinary afternoon dress would do quite well for tonight.'

'In that case I've got a dress with me that will do.' Jo gave a small sigh of relief. She felt at quite bad enough disadvantage at Penderick House as it was, without her clothes letting her down. Her wardrobe was small, but it was versatile, and of good quality. 'I'll have a quick bath first,' she accepted Hannah's offer, and after a few moments' hesitation she washed her hair as well. The smell of the plaster dust from the collapsed ceiling at the cottage seemed to linger, and in the centrally heated bedroom she had been given it would dry sufficiently to be presentable before she went down for the meal.

'This is supposed to have something called crushability.' Jo fished out a guinea-gold, long-sleeved wool dress, and saw to her relief that it lived up to the makers' claim—it was as creaseless as when it was packed. 'It will do for tonight.' She wouldn't need to bother for more than one night, but she did not say so to Hannah.

'It looks lovely with your colouring.' The older woman zipped her up and hooked the roll collar at the back so that it fitted snugly against her throat, and watched as Jo clipped on a bracelet of warm-coloured brown and cream shaded stone set in a silver mount. A large oval brooch of the same opaque stone set off the shoulder of her dress, and drew a complimentary remark from Julian when she sat down at the table.

'It's home-made, I designed it myself,' she said, surprised at his obviously genuine admiration. His own slender tie clip was of solid gold.

'You've got real talent,' Lance Penderick finished his soup with the enthusiasm of hunger, and smiled across at

Jo. 'You could start a cottage industry,' he suggested interestedly. 'The shops here, even those at Arlmouth, don't
offer much for the holidaymakers except bric-à-brac. You'd
do a good trade, I imagine.'

'Chris suggested something of the sort,' Jo smiled back.
She liked Lance. He was almost a replica of Dan to look at,
but much younger, and a good deal less forbidding. At
nearly twenty he already showed signs of his older brother's
tough strength, but thankfully from Jo's point of view he
still retained the uncomplicated friendliness of youth. Dan,
she knew, was twenty-eight, and Julian well into his thir-
ties. She smiled as she recalled Hannah's graphic explana-
tion of the disparity in the brothers' ages.

'Lovelace Penderick was more explorer than sailor. He
was their father,' Hannah pointed to the picture of a dark-
visaged, bearded man hung in the hall as she showed Jo the
way to the dining room. 'He used to be away from home for
years on end sometimes, until he finally came back and
started the canning factory. It gave him an interest to
occupy his time and provided employment for the local
people. There were a lot out of work hereabouts at the
time.'

It explained the beautiful furniture and rugs, Jo thought,
as the portrait hung beside it explained Julian's colouring.
He took after his mother. Her fair, painted face reflected
even from the canvas the fragility that must have made her
wonder how it was she subsequently bore two such strap-
ping sons as Dan and Lance.

'They don't need to work, but they're just like their
father for that. Must occupy themselves.' Hannah shook her
head. 'Mr Julian likes to keep his hands on the reins at the
canning factory. He's got a good manager, so the job isn't
too strenuous for him. And the two young ones,' Jo smiled
at her description of Dan and Lance, but understandingly.
No doubt they would always remain 'the young ones' to

Hannah. 'Well, Lovelace Penderick was just the same. Got the sea in his blood, and must have a deck under his feet, and they're as bad. They're never really happy unless they're out in a boat, and them with a whole fleet to do their bidding. But I wouldn't have them any different. There now, I'm gossiping away,' she became brisk, 'and you waiting for your dinner.'

'Come, you must eat properly. It will help you to get over the shock.' In an unobtrusive manner, Julian kept her plate supplied, making sure, too, that Chris on his other side was similarly attended to. Not by word or gesture did he refer to her breakdown when she arrived, and Jo felt grateful for his consideration. When Dan mentioned the insurance for the cottage, Julian nodded, but refused to be drawn into discussion.

'The insurance is quite in order,' he told her, 'but we'll talk about it tomorrow. Or the next day. When you're more rested.' In his quiet way he was as insistent as Dan that she should stay, and Jo began to feel vaguely trapped. Dan she could defy—would enjoy defying, she told herself, feeling his keen gaze on her face from the other side of the table, and wishing he would either join in the conversation or look away from her. She found his silent regard disconcerting. Her defiance of him up to now had not met with any success, she realised ruefully. He had even brought her luggage up to Penderick House. In all fairness, she had probably been fast asleep at the time, and it was considerate of Dan not to disturb her to ask if she wanted her things collected, or left where they were until she had found other accommodation, but just the same his assumption that he could deal with her belongings as he thought fit without first consulting her rankled badly.

She felt a quick flash of irritation as she looked at him now. Even at the dinner table he had to be different, to be the one standing out. Julian and Lance were in lounge suits, comfortably attired for the evening, but Dan was still in the clothes he wore when he came to the cottage during the morning. True, he had removed the blue jersey, and compromised by slipping a lightweight wool jerkin over his shirt sleeves, as if he did not think her presence at the table was worth while dressing for, and wanted to impress that fact on her without actually saying so.

'What was the catch like this morning?' He spoke directly to Lance, who interrupted his discussion with Chris on fishing to answer.

'Good,' he said laconically, 'and I must say,' he smiled with a hint of malice in his tone, 'the *Kittiwake* behaves like a lady, even with strange hands at the wheel.'

'I told you to let Amos take her out.' Dan's face darkened like a thundercloud, and Jo held her breath. By some means she could not fathom the younger man seemed to be needling his brother, and Dan's reaction was instantaneous. 'I've told you before, the *Kittiwake*'s my boat, and I won't have you skippering her. Not until you're more experienced, anyway,' he compromised ungraciously.

'And how can I get experience, when you consistently refuse to let me take a boat out?' Lance's smile faded, and mounting anger took the place of the teasing. They glared at one another across the table, forgetful of everything, even their guest, and watching them Jo thought how very much alike they were. 'I'm not a child, although you insist on treating me like one.' Lance's voice rose, and he had obvious difficulty in controlling it from breaking into a shout.

'Can't you see Lance is only teasing? He didn't take the *Kittiwake* out, Amos did,' Julian's voice cut across their antagonism. 'And you forget—both of you—that we have a guest.' His voice was curt, but effective. With a surprised stare in his direction Dan and Lance subsided and after a moment they both began eating again. The gentle Julian had asserted himself. If what Melanie had told her was correct, it was a happening unusual enough in itself to warrant instant attention from his two brothers.

'Now you've come to live among a seafaring community, you'll soon learn that a boat is almost like a wife to a man,' Julian smiled at Jo, covering the awkward moment, and to her relief she saw his two brothers relax. Hannah appeared, creating a further diversion with the sweet.

'I don't know if I've got time,' Dan glanced at the clock on the mantelshelf as she put a tray containing five bowls of delicious-looking soufflé on the sideboard.

'That clock's twenty minutes fast.' Hannah clicked her tongue vexedly. 'I moved it when I dusted the shelf this afternoon, and I didn't notice it had stopped until later. It'll have to strike the hour now before I can put it right.'

'This is scrumptious!' Chris dug his spoon into his bowl and grinned his enjoyment of the contents.

'With a recommendation like that, I'm glad the clock is fast,' Dan laughed, and started on his own dish with similar relish, and Jo felt a flash of envy. Lucky Hannah! At least she did not lack appreciation.

'I won't stay for coffee, though,' Dan decided. 'I'll have a drink later on tonight.' Regretfully he emptied his bowl and stood up. 'If you'll excuse me...' He rose and made his excuses, and he was already peeling off his jerkin before he reached the door, as if he could not get out of the room fast enough, thought Jo.

'Your jersey's on the stand, Mr Dan,' she heard Hannah address him as he reached the hall. 'And I've put a snap in a box on the side.'

'You spoil us, Hannah.' For a moment his voice was caressing, its tone almost like Julian's and showing a side to Dan Penderick she had not suspected. Jo listened unashamedly, wondering at the chameleon aspect of this man's moods. She had caught a glimpse of his softer side—but only a glimpse—after the cottage had collapsed, but it had no sooner shown that it was hidden again, so that she wondered afterwards if it had been there at all.

'I'll bring you back a nice breakfast,' Dan promised his housekeeper, and through the partly open door Jo saw him stoop and kiss her on the forehead. 'Goodnight,' he bade her. 'We shouldn't be late in.'

'See that you make it a nice plaice,' Hannah bade him. 'I'm fair sick of pilchards and herrings.'

Dan turned at her parting shot and grinned. 'I'll hook one specially for you,' he promised, and was gone. Where? Surely not birdwatching at this time of night? Jo discounted his teasing about the fish. It had sounded more like a parting ritual than a real promise. But he must be intending to remain out for some hours, or why had Hannah packed him up a 'snap', as she called it? Jo gave up and turned her attention to Dan's two brothers. It was really no concern of hers where Dan was going to, or how long he intended to be away.

'The fish was delicious,' she expressed her appreciation of the meal. 'I don't think I've ever tasted nicer.' It wasn't merely Hannah's cooking, either. There was something else . . .

'It was only caught about an hour before you ate it,' Lance supplied the answer. 'By my own fair hands,' he added with a grin, and Chris looked up interestedly.

'I didn't see you carrying any rods when you came in,' he remarked.

'I didn't catch the plaice with a rod and line. It came in with the net over the side of the *Kittwake*,' he explained. 'She's a trawler, the same as the rest of our fleet,' he mentioned one obvious source of Penderick wealth carelessly. 'I picked it out from among the pilchards specially for our guests.' He bowed gallantly towards Jo, and for some reason she felt glad that Dan had left the table. His black scowl flashed uncomfortably across her mind's eye at Lance's extravagant behaviour, and silently she derided herself for her relief that Dan was not a witness.

Anyone would think I was afraid of him, she jeered at herself, and refused to listen to a small voice which told her that, having incurred Dan's wrath twice during the short time since they had become acquainted, she did not relish doing so again.

'Dan won't be happy until he's taken the *Kittiwake* out again and made sure for himself we didn't hole her on the Claw this morning.' Exasperation tinged Lance's voice, and Jo said,

'Surely he isn't taking his boat out tonight? It's been dark for over an hour, now.'

'There'll be half the fleet out tonight,' Lance answered her. 'They'll be hunting herring,' he waxed informative. 'That's why Dan didn't change out of his working clothes when he came in to dinner,' he added. 'They sail with the tide. It's running full at seven o'clock.' The clock on the mantelshelf said twenty past.

So that was why dinner was linked with the tide. Enlightenment told Jo something else. Dan had changed for dinner, or at least had bothered to put a decent jerkin over his working clothes so that he did not appear in full working gear in front of his guests. She bit her lip, feeling guilty at her hasty judgment of him.

'I'd never thought of fishing as hunting,' Chris harked back to Lance's earlier remark. 'I suppose it is, in a way,' he said thoughtfully.

'It's the old story of the predator chasing prey,' Lance said lightly, 'so it's got to be hunter and hunted, hasn't it?' Thoughtfully, he brought it down to Chris's level of understanding.

Hunter and hunted ... Why should a casual remark of Lance's bring to her mind Dan's silent regard across the dinner table? Jo wondered irritably. She resented the habit he seemed to have made of intruding into her very thoughts. To shut him out, she spoke.

'I didn't realise you fished at night as well as during the day?'

'Dan would have gone out this morning, but...' Lance stopped abruptly, checked by his eldest brother's glare.

'But he came to rescue me instead,' Jo realised with dismay. 'And now he's losing his night's sleep, as well as his day's fishing.' He could have slept during the afternoon, but he had gone to fetch her luggage from the station. Remorse at her lack of charity towards the absent fisherman made her face go pink.

'You didn't hole Dan's boat, I hope?' To cover her confusion she spoke lightly. She already felt the burden of obligation to Dan Penderick too heavy for her liking, and with each minute there seemed some new revelation of what he had done on her behalf, sacrificing his own interests in the process.

'I wouldn't have dared come in to dinner if I had,' Lance laughed.

'You said something about a claw?' Chris's thirst for sensation was typical of his age group. 'It sounded sinister.'

'It is.' Lance did not laugh now, and at his tone the boy's eager interest turned to sober attention. 'I meant the Claw Rocks,' he went on, 'they lie just off the point of Penderick Head. That's the strip of land this house is built on,' he explained. 'It narrows just beyond the few fields that border the gardens, and runs like a thin finger right out to sea. Just past where it ends, there's a string of jagged rocks sticking out of the water. In silhouette, they're not unlike a claw to look at, hence the name. And they're a menace to shipping,' he told his interested audience. 'There's more than one vessel foundered on them. There's a light on the end of Penderick Head now as a warning.'

'D'you mean a real lighthouse? With a lighthouse keeper?'

'No,' Lance smiled at the youngster's enthusiasm. 'I'm sorry to disappoint you, but it's an automatic light. But it's mentioned on the charts, I'll show you where it is on them if you like.' With kindly patience he reached down a chart from a rolled stack on the bookcase and unrolled it on the rug and pointed out the spot. 'But you can walk out there and see for yourself. Oh, it's quite safe,' he assured Jo, catching her silent shake of the head. 'There's a path right along the headland to the end. It's an easy stroll,' he tactfully indicated that it would be within Chris's capabilities, 'and a pleasant one on a nice day.'

'If it's fine tomorrow morning,' Jo gave in to the boy's hopeful pleas without too much coaxing. It would get her out of the house before Dan came back from his fishing trip, and with any luck by the time he had rested—even he would have to sleep some time, she thought caustically, unable to quite control the exasperation that his image raised—she and Chris would be departed to lodgings in the village, and she would feel as if she was her own mistress again.

'Does the fleet fish near the Claw Rocks?' She could not help a tiny shiver of apprehension as she said goodnight to Julian and Lance later, and prepared to carry her bedtime drink upstairs to her room. She did not doubt Dan's capabilities as master of his boat. He would not doubt his own, she thought drily. But what if there was a storm? Momentary fear caught at her throat, and her tone appealed for reassurance.

'Heavens, no, they'll be way beyond the Claw by now.'

'But you said they were inshore boats?' Brought up among an agricultural community as she was, Jo's ignorance of the coast except for brief holidays was abysmal, and drew a chuckle of amusement from Julian.

'I know, but that doesn't mean they fish near the beach,' he smiled. 'They'll be hunting a couple of miles or so out to sea. It's only when they're coming into harbour that they have to pass close to the Claw Rocks, and with good visibility there's no danger. Even in fog, don't forget they've got radar to help them nowadays,' he reminded her.

'Look out of your bedroom window before you go to sleep,' Lance suggested. 'You'll be able to see where the fleet is by their lights.'

It would be like searching for a needle in a haystack, thought Jo with a smile, to find a light among the vast expanse of water beyond the headland, but in case Lance asked her the next morning she obediently switched off her light and drew the curtains back—and blinked in surprise. Across the dark water a string of lights glittered, right out to sea, shimmering like crystals in an arc that crossed the horizon beyond the bay in a seemingly endless line. From this distance they appeared to be stationary, but she knew that if they were trawling the boats must be moving, if only slowly. And on one of them, Dan would be at the wheel, his dark face serious with concentration on his task, all thoughts of the shore—and of herself—expelled from his mind by the need to fill his nets with the harvest the sea provided, and bring home the promised plaice to Hannah. Jo smiled softly into the darkness as she sipped her warm milk. She had no doubt that by some means Dan would keep his promise, and discovered as she fell asleep that however much she resented the skipper of the *Kittiwake* intruding on her thoughts, the fact that his work could exclude her from them left a small corner of desolation in her heart such as even her recent broken engagement could not bring.

'It isn't raining any more, Jo.' Chris gave a preliminary thump on her bedroom door the next morning, and came in fully dressed. He looked as if he had been up for ages. 'You said we could go to the end of the headland 'n' see the Claw Rocks, 'n' the light. I'll know where to look, Lance showed me where they were on the chart,' he said confidently.

'The minute breakfast's over,' Jo promised, hiding her smile. From Lance's description of the headland it was so narrow at the tip there would be no need for them to search, the objects of their walk would be self-evident. And she was as keen to go out as Chris, if only to be missing when Dan got back.

There were three places laid at the breakfast table when she got down, and her eyes looked silent enquiry at Hannah.

'Are we late?' Hannah had said eight o'clock, and it was only five minutes to now.

'No, Mr Julian never bothers with more than a cup of coffee first thing,' Hannah told her calmly, 'and Mr Lance has been down at the harbour supervising the unloading of the boats for the past hour. He had his meal early, and I expect he'll be going out with one of the boats on the morning tide. The other place is for Mr Dan, he'll be back when they've unloaded, for his own meal and a sleep, I expect.'

In that case she would get through her own breakfast and be gone, decided Jo, starting on her cereal without delay. 'We'll go for our walk,' she told Chris, 'the weather may not last,' she blackmailed him into not lingering over his own breakfast, and without much delay, though to her strained nerves it seemed to take twice as long as usual, she was able to quit the table and get ready to go out. But she was not quick enough to miss Dan.

'Did you sleep well?' he asked, bumping into her in the hall. His keen eyes raked her face, taking in her bright eyes and the faint flush of colour in her cheeks that had not been there the day before, and was heightened now because he watched her, and deepened rapidly because she was annoyed to find herself flushing. He seemed to have the most disconcerting effect on her, she thought crossly. After being accustomed to meeting literally hundreds of men in the form of her father's students, for as long as she could remember, it seemed silly to let a virtual stranger put her out of countenance like this.

'Very well, thank you.' She sounded like a small girl being polite, and his lips twitched slightly. 'Did you manage to bring Hannah her plaice?' she could not resist asking him, and the twitch became an amused smile.

'Oh yes, I managed to find one to suit her,' he assured Jo. 'Two, for good measure,' he added, his eyes twinkling.

'She's waiting to give you your breakfast.' For some reason Jo did not want to tell him she was going out. She had the uncomfortable feeling he might try to stop her from leaving, though she was a free agent, she told herself firmly, he could not make her remain if she did not want to stay.

'I've just told her not to bother, I had some on the boat after we finished unloading.'

'We're going to see the Claw Rocks 'n' the light at the end of the headland.' Jo could cheerfully have slapped Chris, but it was too late now, Dan knew where they were going, and she automatically tensed, waiting—expecting— him to obstruct their plans. But he only said mildly, 'I'll come with you, it's a nice walk, and I could do with stretching my legs after a night on the boat. That is, if you don't mind the smell of fish?' He was still in his working clothes, that must have been covered with something while he was out, Jo judged, for they were still clean and dry, and despite his half apology did not smell at all fishy.

'We shan't trespass,' she assured him hurriedly. 'Lance and Julian both said it was all right to go.' He need not think she was trying to pry round his home. Her chin came up in an automatic gesture of defence, but he merely said calmly:

'That's O.K., you can go anywhere you like. You're a

member of the household now,' he reminded her, and Jo flashed him a quick glance. He returned her look with an unfathomable expression in his eyes. She wished she knew what he was thinking, and then she was glad she did not. Dan's attitude to herself was disconcerting enough without probing further, she decided.

'We were just going up to get a woolly each.' She nearly said 'my mac', but remembered in time where she had left it. She did not quite know what to do about that. It was a problem she would have to sort out during the day. The fact that the only cash she possessed was in the pocket worried her. Even to get into the bank at Arlmouth she would need bus fares, and pride forbade that she borrowed from the Pendericks. She annexed Chris and made for the stairs. If they took their time sorting out a jersey each, maybe Dan would get tired of waiting and leave them to their walk in peace.

'Slip your mac on,' she told her brother. Fortunately he had been wearing it when he went out with Melanie the day before, and she would manage somehow, herself. 'I'll make do with my anorak.'

'Your mac would be warmer.' Chris strolled through into her room, buttoning up his own waterproof. 'Here it is, I'll get it for you.' He crossed the carpet and reached up to the hook behind her bedroom door. 'You won't need your purse with you, will you?' he asked innocently. 'It's heavy—look, it makes the pocket bulge.' He held out Jo's mac towards her. The red mac, that she had left hanging behind the door of the cottage living room, where Dan had forbidden her to enter to retrieve it, because of the danger of being trapped in another rock fall.

CHAPTER FOUR

'You might have been killed!'

She felt angry. Angry, and frightened at the thought of Dan risking his life to rescue her mac.

'It wasn't worth it. You forbade me to try,' she reminded him, visibly upset, and angry with herself for showing it.

'The rock fall had settled overnight. If there were going to be any more immediate falls, they would have come by the morning,' he brushed aside her thanks, 'and I'm familiar with the cliffs, I'd know whether it was safe to go into the cottage or stay out,' he defended his action gruffly. 'Look, there's a kittiwake, the bird my boat's named after.' He directed Chris's attention out over the water, deliberately changing the subject.

'I left my bird book in the cottage.' Chris waited for them to catch up. 'I'll have to get another one when we go to Arlmouth.'

'I didn't notice a book,' Dan said, 'though I brought what I could find from your bedrooms while I was about it,' he told Jo casually. 'It's lucky your luggage was still at the station,' he remarked.

'There's the light—look! I can see it flashing,' Chris called their attention excitedly to where the beam from the end of the headland swung in a regular arc, and his enthusiastic chatter saved Jo from replying. She would have found it difficult anyway. The thought that Dan had risked going into the cottage sent her cold all over. He would not have known about her mac being there at all if she had not mentioned going back for it. If he had been injured, it would have been her fault. She shivered, and cuddled closer into the red garment that she found she disliked more than ever now. She heartily wished she had bought the blue one.

'Are you cold?' The skipper of the *Kittiwake* looked as if heat and cold were alike a matter of indifference to him. The sleeves of his jersey were pushed up to the elbows despite the keen morning breeze, that had not yet mellowed to springtime warmth.

'No, I was thinking of what Lance said about those rocks,' she lied, unwilling to reveal her real thoughts to him. She nodded towards the line of spear-sharp points jutting cruelly from the water, and visible as they approached the end of the headland.

'The Claw Rocks? They look even more menacing from the sea.' Dan's face sobered as Lance's had done when he spoke of them, and he gazed at the jagged outcrop reflectively.

'Then I'm glad I'm only looking at them from the land,' Jo said fervently.

'You'll have to see them from the water one day.' Julian joined them, he must have followed them out and taken his own time in catching them up. Although he walked well enough, his movements were necessarily slow. Dan looked at him in surprise.

'Aren't you going to the canning plant this morning?'

'Later on,' Julian replied equably. 'I thought I'd have a stroll first.'

It only needs Lance to join us now, thought Jo with sudden amusement. It was obvious from the surprise evinced by each of the brothers at the other's presence on the headland at this hour in the morning that such delinquency from their normal duties was the exception rather than the rule. Having house guests had upset the routine of the Pendericks in more ways than one, she thought with a touch of malice, and it was their own fault it had happened. She had not wanted to come. Did not want—had no intention, she corrected her own thoughts—of staying.

'Have you ever been out on a fishing vessel?' Julian asked Chris kindly, and as the boy shook his head, 'Why not take them out with you on the *Kittiwake* tomorrow?' he asked Dan. 'The weather's set fair, and it's not unduly cold.'

'Ooh, can we? D'you really mean...' Chris could not believe his good fortune, and his face shone with anticipation.

'Dan may not want to...' Jo began dubiously. If Dan agreed to take them out, it would mean they would have to remain at Penderick House for another day and night longer. But perhaps Dan would not agree. She stole a glance at his face. He did not look as if he favoured the suggestion. Indeed, his expression was openly reluctant, and Jo flushed uncomfortably.

'Perhaps some other time,' she tried again.

'Lance can crew for me.' Dan seemed suddenly to make up his mind about something, and added obliquely, 'Amos can take the *Sea Swallow* out.'

'Don't let us put you to any inconvenience.' Jo cut short her brother's unrestrained whoop of delight.

'You won't.' Dan glanced at her briefly, and then away again, and Jo suddenly felt snubbed. His tone suggested that if she was of the slightest inconvenience, he would not have agreed to take her.

'I don't believe it.' Lance gazed at Jo incredulously as he paused for a moment in his task of supervising the unloading of the day's catch later that afternoon. Jo had acted on Julian's second suggestion a lot more willingly than she had received his first.

'The boats that went out on the early tide will be back by the afternoon,' he told her. 'You'll have time to watch them unload if you're interested, and still be back in plenty of time for dinner.'

That meant she need not see Dan again until the evening meal. Jo grasped at Julian's suggestion with as much enthusiasm as Chris, but for an entirely different reason, and paused in the act of knotting a scarf over her head to foil the mischievous wind. Why was she perpetually looking for an avenue of escape from Dan Penderick? she wondered in exasperation, and then, scornfully, gave herself an easy answer. She did not want to intrude where she was not wanted. But it was Dan who had brought her to Penderick House, almost by force, and certainly against her will. And it was at Dan's insistence, as well as Julian's, that she was being obliged to stay. He had called her a member of the household, and seemed to regard herself and Chris as fixtures for the time being. She shrugged her thoughts away impatiently.

'He said you'd crew for him, and Amos could take the *Sea Swallow* out,' Chris said importantly. 'Shall we be able to crew for him as well?' he asked hopefully.

'Well, I'm...!' For a second Lance's face took on a thunderous expression, making his likeness to Dan even more marked, Jo thought, and then his look cleared, and he laughed. 'We might let you off crewing for this trip,' he told Chris gravely, subduing his mirth with an effort. 'Roddy will help out I expect, unless Amos insists on taking him along on the *Sea Swallow*.'

'We seem to be causing everyone a lot of trouble.' The cause of Lance's amusement was not obvious to Jo, and it began to irritate her.

'You're not,' he assured her, seeming to sense her feelings. In one way Lance was a bit like Julian; he had some of the older man's sensitivity, Jo thought. 'It's only that Amos is so superstitious it's just not true, particularly in this day and age,' he explained with a twinkle, 'and Dan goes out of his way not to upset him. He's the oldest skipper in the fleet. Dan doesn't believe in all that rubbish himself, of course,' he added, and his grin broadened.

'What rubbish?' Jo was more puzzled than ever.

'Sorry, I forgot you were a landlubber,' Lance laughed cheerfully. 'Women are supposed to be bad luck on the fishing boats,' he explained, 'and you,' he added unnecessarily, 'are a woman,' his glance adding that he was flatteringly glad of the fact.

'Are you superstitious?' Jo was too modern to regard the whole thing as anything more than sheer nonsense, and she spoke lightly.

'No, I'm just glad of any diversion on a working trip,' Lance responded in the same vein, and added, 'particularly a nice-looking diversion,' with just the right amount of teasing in his voice for Jo not to mind, even though her colour rose in its usual traitorous manner. 'There's Amos now,' Lance nodded towards a blue-jerseyed figure perched on a post by the harbour wall, with the folds of a fishing net hung up in front of him. 'Come and say hello,' he signalled the men loading the lorries with fish boxes, each one Jo noticed with the picture of a tern sketched along its side, and one of them took his place as he strolled away with Jo and Chris towards the white-haired fisherman, who had a stubby pipe stuck out sideways from his face in a way that reminded Jo irresistibly of Popeye.

'Jo and Chris are staying with us for the time being,' Lance introduced them.

'I'd heard.' The gnarled hands continued their task of mending the torn net, uninterrupted by the arrival of strangers, although a pair of shrewd blue eyes took in their presence, and, thought Jo uncomfortably, everything about them at the same time, in the one swift glance.

'Isn't the string thin?' Chris said interestedly. 'It doesn't look strong enough to hold fish, somehow.'

'It's not string, it's one of the new man-made fibres, they're finer and stronger,' Lance explained.

'It looks tough.' Jo reached out to finger the fold of net nearest to her.

'Doan'ee touch it!' She pulled her hand back hastily at the old fisherman's sharp rebuff, and coloured furiously. 'I'm sorry,' she stammered, 'I didn't mean ...'

'It's unlucky for a woman to touch the nets,' Lance said quietly, and Jo noticed that in front of Amos he did not show any sign of amusement.

'Well, I didn't touch it,' she assured him tartly, 'though since I haven't got long blonde hair, I can't be a mermaid, so I don't see why I'm supposed to be unlucky.'

'Doan mock at things 'ee knows nothin' about,' the old man growled, and Jo looked up at Lance helplessly.

'I'll run you back to the house in my car, if you'll wait,' he helped her out generously. 'There's a seat out of the wind further along the harbour wall.' Tactfully he ushered her away, and once they were at a safe distance Jo grimaced ruefully.

'That wasn't a huge success,' she admitted. 'It's a good job you didn't tell him Dan is taking us out on the *Kittiwake.*'

'Dan can do that himself,' Lance grinned. 'But here's someone else you can make friends with.' He waved cheerfully to a dark-haired girl strolling along with a basket in her hand. 'Have you got what you wanted?' he asked her as they drew closer, and she nodded.

'Amos saw me right,' she indicated her basket, and Jo saw it was full of fish. Evidently the girl did her shopping direct from the suppliers, she thought with a smile. If the fish at dinner the evening before was anything to go by, it was the best way.

'You haven't met Tessa, have you?' Lance asked Jo. 'This is Melanie's sister,' he identified her, 'and this is Jo Wallace,' he chatted on in a friendly fashion, and Jo smiled at the other girl. She was about her own age, maybe a year younger, and as lovely in a more mature way as Melanie. She had the same long black hair and huge black eyes, though in the older girl's face there was a hint of haughty temper that could have been the result of her being spoilt because of her beauty. Jo had noticed it before in exceptionally handsome people, a flaw that marred what could otherwise have been perfection, she thought sadly.

'Jo Wallace?' The girl looked puzzled, and ignored Jo's outstretched hand. 'I thought when Melanie brought that bauble home,' her voice was scornful of the pretty pendant Jo had so painstakingly made for the younger girl, 'it was an artist and his brother who'd taken the cottage.'

'You thought she was a fellow?' Lance grinned delightedly. 'Heaven forbid,' he said fervently, and the other girl scowled.

'It's a reasonable mistake, with a name like that.'

'It's one that's been made before,' Jo admitted with a sigh. 'It's short for Joanne.'

'Then why on earth don't you call yourself by your proper name, then everybody will know who you are,' Tessa snapped ungraciously.

She's disappointed I'm not another man, Jo thought shrewdly. In a small community it would be another conquest for a girl like Tessa. She knew a swift hope that Melanie's young innocence would not end up like the petulant beauty before her.

'There's Chris, down by the boats,' Lance pointed to where the boy sat swinging his heels from the bollard, absorbed in the activity confronting him.

'Melanie said there was a boy. A child,' Tessa said indifferently. Chris was too young to be of any interest to her yet. 'At least when she's running around playing with him she's not under my feet.' It sounded as if even her sister, young as she was, might be regarded as a rival. Jo found herself disliking Melanie's sister, and wondered why she had hoped they might be friends. Tessa Tremayne was not the type to welcome friends of her own sex.

'I know which one the *Kittiwake* is, Jo,' Chris came trotting back—he could manage to run, now, for short distances, an achievement he was inordinately proud of. 'I'll show you if you like, then you'll know which boat we're going out on tomorrow. Oh, sorry,' as it dawned on him that his sister had company.

'You're going out on the *Kittiwake*?' Tessa looked as incredulous as Lance had done. 'You can't mean Dan's taking *you* out with him?' Strangely, her emphasis did not sound insulting, just disbelieving. Tessa was a child of the coast, and knew the ways of the fishermen.

'Yes, but Amos isn't crewing for him. He's putting up with me instead,' Lance grinned. 'And we hope Amos will let Roddy come with us as well.'

'Does Amos know?' Tessa's voice was slightly awed, and Jo felt a surge of impatience. From the way these people were behaving, she thought crossly, anyone would think she possessed the evil eye.

'No, Dan will tell him.' Lance's tone added 'thank goodness'. 'I've been telling Jo how superstitious Amos is.'

'Then if you know how much trouble you're causing, surely you'll stay off the boat,' Tessa rounded on Jo sharply. 'You'll probably be sick anyway, most trippers are,' she said scornfully.

'She's not a tripper, she's a resident,' Lance said quietly, and underneath his easy manner there was a faint hint of warning, which Tessa chose to ignore.

'A resident?' the other girl sneered. 'Resident where? At the cottage on the cliff?' She must know by now it was uninhabitable.

'No, at Penderick House,' Lance replied, and now there was a touch of steel in his voice, but Tessa did not seem to hear it.

'Oh, trust Dan to collect all the flotsam and jetsam,' she snapped. 'He's too soft-hearted for his own good. Perhaps now you'll go back inland where you came from,' she said to Jo unpleasantly. 'Keep the coast for a day trip to Blackpool, and leave living here to those who belong.' She swung on her heel, and with an indifferent toss of her head strode away towards a small van parked close by. Jo noticed it had the name of her father's flower farm emblazoned on the side.

'We might as well be off, too.' Lance looked faintly uncomfortable. 'My car's over here.' He led the way in the opposite direction to where the van was parked, and Jo called Chris to them. 'We're ready to go.' He came willingly enough, certain in the knowledge that he would be back the following day, and tucked himself in the back of the car where he could gaze out of the rear window at the fascinating new world of the harbour. They passed the van on their way. Jo was surprised to find it still parked there, from the way Tessa had flounced off she gave the impression that she could not get away fast enough, but Jo caught sight of her black hair and swinging basket walking back along the harbour wall. She thought nothing of it until Dan joined them for dinner, with knitted brows and a look of angry impatience on his face.

'Couldn't you have left it to me to tell Amos to take out the *Sea Swallow* for us tomorrow?' he growled at Lance as soon as they were seated.

'I haven't said anything to Amos,' Lance looked taken aback at the thrust. 'Jo told me you were taking her and Chris out with you, and wanted me to crew for you. I don't remember you saying anything to Amos either, did you, Jo?' he asked her, so obviously at a loss that even Dan seemed convinced.

'Not I,' denied Jo firmly. 'Amos didn't like me as it was,' she remembered ruefully. 'And I know Chris didn't say anything. And Julian's the only other one who knows we're going out, unless...' She stopped, remembering Tessa Tremayne.

'We met Tessa. I introduced her to Jo, and Chris came up and mentioned you were taking them out on the *Kittiwake*.' Lance latched on to Joe's thoughts without any trouble.

'Tessa wouldn't say anything to Amos, she knows how he'd react unless he was told in the right way,' Dan scotched the suggestion, but Jo did not feel so sure. Tessa Tremayne did not like her, she had made that obvious, and probably—Jo suspected her guess was not far wrong— Tessa liked Dan more than a little. Lance was too young for her to be interested in, and Julian—somehow, one could not imagine Julian being married. His disabilities had turned an already gentle, academic nature into one that retreated into the world of books and music, and was made utterly content thereby. No, of the three it would be Dan who would attract Tessa Tremayne. They deserved one another, thought Jo unfairly, and wished heartily Julian had not suggested them going on the fishing trip in the first place.

Nevertheless she could not help feeling excited as they stepped out of the car the following morning and stood waiting for Dan to park it and join them.

'The *Kittiwake*'s tied up at the far end of the harbour wall,' he told Lance. 'It's a good way to walk, but I thought it would be easier for Jo to get aboard.'

'He's letting you off lightly,' Lance quipped. 'You'll be walking down a flight of nice safe stone steps straight on to the deck, instead of climbing up a rope ladder and scrambling over the side, the same as he would have made me do.' He tried in vain to look hard done by, and caused a laugh all round; even Dan seemed to be in a cheerful mood. Chris stuck to him like a leech. Jo had heard Dan talking to the boy before breakfast, and was glad she overheard their conversation. Their host evidently took his responsibilities seriously, because in return for the trip he was demanding instant obedience from Chris while he was on board, a promise which the boy eagerly gave, and was rewarded by being nominated a member of the crew for the day. Jo smiled as she listened. However prickly Dan might be with grown-ups, he had a wonderful way with children, and she felt relaxed and at ease, knowing the boy to be in safe hands. Having sole responsibility for his welfare had sometimes weighed heavily upon her during the last few months.

'I'll go first, the steps might be slippery.' Dan turned down the narrow flight of steps at the end of the harbour wall, and held up his hand. 'Hold on to me,' he told Jo, then as she hesitated, 'I don't want you dropping over the side before we even start off. Lance will do the same for Chris.' His voice was an order rather than a comment, and she automatically put her hand into his, feeling the strong grip of his fingers about her own. With Dan holding on to her, the steps suddenly looked twice as broad, and she began to descend with more confidence. A quick glance behind her showed Lance with Chris in tow in a similar manner. Dan's homily about obeying orders had gone home, she thought thankfully. 'Now, stand still for a moment,' Dan told her as they reached a step level with the deck of the boat, that sidled restlessly with the swell up and down against the sheltering stones, like a thoroughbred eager to be away. Without saying what he meant to do Dan straddled widely, placing one foot on the deck and the other on the stone step. Without a pause he reached out and grasped Jo firmly round the waist and swung her down safely on to the gently rocking deck, holding on to her hand for another moment to make sure she was steady, before he let her go into the keeping of a tousled, grinning lad not much older than Melanie, whose shock of red hair seemed strangely out of place in their dun-coloured surroundings.

'I'm Roddy. O.K., Skipper, I've got her,' he introduced himself, and took firm hold of Jo at one and the same time, and pulled her along the deck for a foot or two to enable Dan to bring both feet on to the *Kittiwake* and help Lance perform a similar service for Chris.

'Our new apprentice,' Dan introduced the boy laconically to Roddy, who grinned in a friendly manner. 'Keep an eye on him,' he instructed the redhead, and for a moment the eyes of the youth and the man met. Roddy nodded. 'He'll be all right with me, Skipper. Come on, young 'un.' With a look of dazed delight on his face Chris stumbled after this new hero, and Jo smiled.

'Thank you.' She looked full at Dan, letting her gratitude show, and for a moment the self-contained sailor looked disconcerted. 'Do I qualify as crew?' Jo asked him meekly, taking pity on his obvious embarrassment.

'You can make the kye. I'll show you what's in the wheelhouse,' he told her gruffly, and took her arm, steadying her as she walked uncertainly for'ard. 'You'll find it helps if you develop a nautical roll,' he said amusedly as she staggered on the shifting boards. 'Stand still for a minute until the *Sea Swallow's* gone past, we're catching her wash.' He stood still himself and drew her to him, keeping her within the circle of his arm as a similar vessel came in close, following the curve of the harbour wall as it headed for the entrance and out to the open sea. The man at the wheel did not even glance in their direction and Jo saw his pipe stuck belligerently from the side of his mouth. Amos made it plain he disapproved of women aboard fishing boats.

'What's kye?' Jo let her ignorance show in order to cover her confusion. Dan's arm round her made her feel sheltered, and safe—and suddenly shy. Lance's mischievous grin did nothing to help, and she wrinkled her nose at him, silently begging him to stop.

'A sort of thick sweet cocoa, with a knob of butter in it

and a lacing of rum.' Dan's deep voice rumbled through his chest, and sent unaccountable tremors through her that she decided she did not want to listen to.

'Ugh!' She brought her attention back to his recipe, and shuddered.

'It helps to keep the cold out when you're gutting fish in a keen wind,' he told her calmly. 'Come on, she's steadier now. If you stay in the wheelhouse, you'll be able to see everything that's going on, and keep warm at the same time,' he told her. 'I'll send Chris in to you now and then, to make sure he does too,' he added.

'Shan't we be in your way?' It rather sounded as if he was parking her out of his way, she thought ruefully, but like Chris she had every intention of doing exactly as she was told while she was aboard the *Kittiwake*. The boat was Dan's world, and on it she acknowledged that as master he had the right to reign supreme. Ashore it was a different matter...

'Once we're out on the grounds you'll have the wheelhouse to yourself,' he told her. 'There's the stove, if you insist on being a member of the crew,' his lips twitched slightly. 'The supplies are in the rack,' he indicated a deep wire basket affair screwed to the bulkhead, 'you'll have to use condensed milk—we don't bother with bottles on board, they're liable to get broken. Oh, and if it gets rough, use the fiddles on the stove, it's safer. Ready to go, Lance?' he stuck his head back through the wheelhouse door, and at Lance's cheery affirmative went to join him and left Jo to sort herself out.

'Fiddles? What fiddles?' She could see nothing that looked remotely like a fiddle. A steady vibration from the deck under her feet told her they were under way, and glancing through the windows of the wheelhouse she could see the harbour wall already beginning to recede. Dan had been right about having a good view, the little enclosure was all glass from about the height of her waist, which took away any claustrophobic effect its size might have had.

'You don't get seasick, I hope?' Dan rejoined her, guiding his boat with a light touch towards the entrance to the harbour.

'I never have been yet.' Sudden doubt assailed her, and she thrust it hastily from her mind. Seasickness was mostly a matter of nerves, she told herself robustly. But it would be just her luck to suffer a baptism while she was in Dan's company. To divert her mind she took stock of the minute wheelhouse. With Dan occupying it as well, his bulk made it look even smaller, and she crouched on the wooden bench type seat running along its length and pulled her feet up under her, so that they occupied as little floor space as possible, and tried not to think of the varied smells that assailed her nostrils. A mixture of salt, tar, fish, and wet oilskins, to say nothing of the acrid reek of diesel oil, would not help if she became queasy.

'I usually keep the door open.' Dan spoke without turning round, his attention occupied on his route. 'It takes off the effect of the engine smells.' He left her to open or close the door if she wanted to, whether from indifference to her comfort or consideration in case she might feel cold she was left to conjecture.

I'll have to ask him what fiddles are, she decided reluctantly at last, occupying the ensuing silence with looking round her. It meant she would have to show her ignorance for the second time, but she discovered she did not care. I'm enjoying myself after all, she realised. In spite of its size, or lack of it, the wheelhouse was a cosy place to be, and at a squeeze there would be room enough for them all if the weather turned really wet.

'The *Kittiwake* isn't as big as I thought it would be.' She had imagined, from the pride with which Dan spoke of his boat, it would be much larger.

'She's under sixty feet long,' he told her. 'There's a local byelaw that forbids a bigger boat from fishing within three miles of the shore, so I keep the fleet below the regulation length, and it gives a greater margin of choice for working, particularly when the shoals come right into the bay. They do sometimes.'

'It still seems small.' She glanced at the seemingly endless expanse of water confronting them as Dan let the spokes of the wheel trickle through his fingers, and put the arms of the harbour gradually astern.

'She only seems small in contrast to her surroundings.' Dan spoke of his boat as if it was a human being. 'If she was in a canal she'd look big enough to you then,' he said with unanswerable logic. 'Don't worry, the Kittiwake can take any weather that's likely to blow up around these coasts,' her master assured Jo confidently.

She was glad to hear it. She was not exactly nervous, she told herself, but her land-bred feet were accustomed to terrain that stood obligingly still, and the Kittiwake was responding to the rhythm of the open sea. In the calm water inside the harbour walls the boat rocked with cradle-like gentleness, but now it shivered like a live thing and lifted its bows eagerly to the oncoming sea, which passed with a hissing rush of water as the vessel pitched.

'We're all set now until we reach the grounds.' Lance poked an enquiring head into the wheelhouse. 'I could do with a cup of tea,' he hinted thirstily.

'I thought you drank—what was it?' Jo tried to remember the name of the revolting mixture Dan had told her about.

'Kye? No, that comes later, when we've finished gutting and stowing,' Lance told her. 'And you won't pull a face like that when you're frozen to the bone and still within hours of home and a fire,' he told her. 'You'll be glad enough to drink a mug of kye then. I'll put the kettle on to boil now,' he offered.

'Jo's in charge of the galley,' Dan told him, 'the water's in that container in the corner. Just turn the tap at the bottom,' he instructed her.

'I'll take that.' Jo swung to her feet and relieved Lance of the kettle. She knelt beside the water container, unsure whether or not to resent what amounted to an order from Dan. She had offered to be part of the crew, and evidently he had taken her at her word.

'I'll let him see I can manage by myself,' she vowed, and reached out hurriedly and grasped the edge of the stove to keep her balance as she stood up again and the boat gave a livelier than usual buck just as she regained her feet.

'Try not to spill the water, it's all we've got to last us until we get ashore again.'

Jo compressed her lips as Dan spoke to her without bothering to turn. He could not possibly have seen the water slop over her hand before she managed to get the lid of the kettle in place, so it must be pure guesswork on his part that she had had a spill. The fact that he guessed correctly annoyed her unreasonably, and he did not miss the opportunity to criticise her, she thought, vexed that he seemed to be making a sport of her difficulty in keeping her balance. She clattered the kettle on to the top of the stove with a feeling of relief at having got it safely where it belonged, and turned to look for a match.

'Watch it!' Dan reached across her and grabbed the kettle as it slid at the behest of the pitching vessel, and would have crashed to the floor, water and all, but for his intervention. 'I told you to use the fiddles.'

'Fiddles mean violins to me,' Jo snapped, her patience running out. 'And it's unreasonable to want cups of tea when nothing will stand still for two minutes together,' she told him blackly. 'Surely it would be easier, and safer, to bring flasks with you? If the kettle had been boiling there could have been a bad accident.' She steadied it as it tried to slide back the other way, and the spout instantly regurgitated some more of its precious contents.

'You've filled it too full.' Dan picked it up and poured half of its contents back into the water container. 'It's better to give the water room to surge, that way you won't get scalded. And the fiddles are to stop it from slipping over the edge of the stove,' he added, reaching down and fishing out some long narrow pieces of metal, which he proceeded to fit into slots along the top of the stove, making a safe barrier several inches high all along the sides.

'I've seen wooden ones used on the table of a cruise liner in rough weather, but I didn't know they were called fiddles.' Enlightenment dawned on Jo as she watched him at work. 'And the liner didn't heave up and down at the same speed as the *Kittiwake* either,' she added critically, resenting what she considered to be his superior attitude to her land-accustomed clumsiness, that made her stagger on the unsteady deck as she released the edge of the stove to give Dan room to put the kettle behind the newly fixed restraints.

'A cruise liner is bigger and heavier than the *Kittiwake*, it would sit lower in the water,' he retorted calmly. 'That would make it more stable.' He reached out and steadied her with his free arm, and used his other hand to lodge the kettle safely on the stove. Unhurriedly he lit the burner underneath it, and when he was satisfied that it was going nicely he clasped his one hand loosely in the other, behind her back. Unresisting, he drew her to him, and looked deep into her startled eyes with an enigmatic smile in his own.

'But it wouldn't be half so much fun,' he said. And kissed her.

CHAPTER FIVE

IT was a tantalising kiss—half jest, half taunt, full on her parted lips, so that her gasp of surprise was stilled to silence by the firm pressure of his own.

For a moment she lay passive in his arms, stunned into immobility by the unexpectedness of his action, and then she stirred, and struggled to break free, and he released her, though he still kept one hand lightly on the stove behind her, so that when she stumbled backwards, caught unawares again by the movement of the boat, she came up against the hard whipcord strength of his arm instead of a sharp corner of the wheelhouse furniture, and did not bruise herself.

'You—you . . . !' she put her hands to her burning cheeks, and choked into indignant silence. Still his blue eyes held her, boring into hers, watching her reaction, and she could not look away. His look mesmerised her, and the bleak grey world of water and sky outside the windows of the wheelhouse, and the presence of the others on the boat, faded into unreality as she stared back at him, trapped by his compelling stare.

Had he ever kissed Tessa Tremayne like this? The question came, she did not know from where, and it should not matter to her. But it did. Had he, perhaps, brought Tessa out with him on the *Kittiwake*, and made love to her? With the boat surrounded by a sheet of inhospitable water, there would be no way she could escape, even if she wanted to. But Tessa would not want to escape, of that she felt sure—and realised with dismay that only half of herself wanted to. The commonsense half, that told her to flee while there was still time, before her throbbing heart became irretrievably tangled in the carelessly flung meshes of this fisherman's net. Part of the flotsam and jetsam that Tessa had accused him of collecting.

Tessa had accused him of being soft-hearted, as well, but Jo did not agree. It was no kindness to her, she thought wretchedly, to casually kiss, and awaken her heart to a swift response when she would fain it had remained free. Now she knew, with a feeling akin to fear, that it would never be wholly free again. Part of it—the sweetest part, that Melvin for some reason had never awakened—would always belong to the master of the *Kittiwake*, and sail with him on his frail barque that his brother had laughingly compared with a wife to its owner. And it would leave herself with only the empty shell of the part that was left, to chart an uncertain course across a sea of future days that suddenly looked bleaker to Jo, and more stormy, than the reality they floated on now.

'Here's Lance, with Chris.' She grasped desperately at the diversion, anything to enable her to break away from Dan's stare. To her relief he turned and looked towards his brother.

'They've come for a cup of tea, I expect, and it's not ready yet.' He made it sound like an accusation of inefficiency, and Jo gritted her teeth. The moment was gone, the sweet, shattering moment between herself and Dan that had lasted for perhaps two minutes, and done damage to her heart that a lifetime would not repair.

'It's almost ready.' The kettle gave a cheery signal just as Lance appeared, pushing Chris in front of him.

'That's the only thing that's allowed to whistle on board,' he told the youngster solemnly. 'If anyone else whistles, it's bad luck.'

'Don't stuff his head full of that nonsense,' Dan said sharply, 'or he'll grow up with as many taboos as Amos. One in the fleet is quite bad enough.' He ladled tea into the pot with an expert hand, and adding water from the noisy kettle, put it back on the stove, safely behind the fiddles. 'Give it a minute to brew, you'll find mugs in the cupboard underneath the seat.'

She delved and discovered half a dozen enamel mugs slotted safely into holes drilled out of a board shelf. For a second her heart misgave her. Everything on board seemed geared to withstand the onslaught of rough water. Except herself and Chris, and if it came the child would probably be more thrilled than afraid. He still retained a sublime faith in the grown-up world that Jo herself no longer shared.

'I'll pour out, you sit down,' Lance took pity on her unsteady stance. 'Chris is finding his sea legs a lot quicker than you are,' he teased.

'That's because my one leg's a bit shorter than the other since the accident.' Chris seemed unaware of the sudden silence that descended on the wheelhouse, and went on matter-of-factly, 'Roddy says it's an advantage really, when the boat tips I can put my longer leg on the bit that goes down, and it helps level me up.' He accepted a half filled mug of generously sugared tea, and looked askance at the door. 'What about Roddy's?' he asked, considerate of his new hero, and innocent of the sudden compassion in the faces of the two men in the wheelhouse, and the quick tears that stung Jo's eyes.

'Roddy will have his tea next.' Dan found his voice first. 'We'll be shooting the nets soon,' he talked on, easing the tension, and accepted his mug, half full the same as the one Chris held. 'It only spills if you fill it to the top.' He glanced across at Jo and she felt a quick flash of vexation. She could have sorted that out for herself, she thought tartly. Dan must think she was witless to need advising on every tiny detail.

'I'll take this one for Roddy.' Lance picked up the last mug and prepared to depart.

'I want you to stay in here as observer.' Dan checked

Chris's move to follow him. 'Keep an eye on the wheel for me, will you?' he asked gravely. 'It should stay steady.' He carefully fixed it so that a hurricane wouldn't shift it, thought Jo, but she said nothing, grateful for his attention to the boy. 'If it shows signs of breaking loose, come and let me know. Oh, and if you kneel on the end of the seat,' he turned in the act of quitting the wheelhouse, 'you'll see everything that's going on. Try and remember what happens, and when you're as big as Roddy you'll know what to do without being told.' He spoke as if he took it for granted that the boy would come out on future trips, and looking at her brother's rapt face as he obediently curled up on the seat and pressed his nose against the glass pane, determined not to miss a move anyone made, Jo realised Dan had just made it even harder for her to leave Penderick House than it had been before.

'I'll throw the tea leaves over the side.' She got to her feet restlessly, seeking movement to steady the turbulent thoughts that went round and round like a whirlpool in her head, almost envying the men their occupation. Dan, she was sure, had forgotten all about her and Chris by now, his back was turned towards them as he bent about some task on deck.

'I'll take your mug back with me when I've got rid of the tea leaves.' She passed Roddy on her way to the rail, and he nodded in a preoccupied fashion.

'Spit first, before you throw them overboard,' he advised.

'Don't be disgusting,' she scolded him, and made for the side. 'I hope Chris doesn't pick up these outlandish superstitions,' she thought fervently, and with a quick, impatient movement she flicked the lid off the teapot and hurled the wet leaves over the rail. Instantly she heard Dan shout, but it was too late to check her movement. 'A few tea leaves won't spoil your fishing,' she muttered rebelliously, but instinctively she turned as he called her name, just in time to prevent the wet tea leaves from blowing back full into her face. As it was they splattered the sleeve of her mac with damp darkness.

'Roddy told you to spit first,' Dan grinned. 'Next time, perhaps you'll listen.' And he turned away, still grinning, his strong hands playing out the net that streamed from the side of the *Kittiwake* and dropped through the water below in silent seeking, to claim its victims from the deep.

Jo shivered, and turned back into the wheelhouse, appreciating Lance's comment fully for the first time. Fishing *was* hunting. And these men were the hunters, their faces keen and absorbed, involved in their task of stalking their prey to the exclusion of everything—and everyone—else. Jo shut the door of the wheelhouse with unnecessary force, thankful to close herself in—and Dan out. He had made cruel jest of her lack of local knowledge. Tessa would doubtless have known not to throw tea leaves over the side of the boat right into the teeth of the wind blowing in the opposite direction. So would I, if I'd thought about it, Jo thought miserably, but she could not undo her action now, and it added another point to the score which Dan seemed to be mounting up against her.

'There must be a kitten on the boat somewhere. Have you seen it, Jo?'

'No.' She looked at Chris in surprise. Surely Dan would not succumb to carrying a black cat for luck, she thought caustically, not after his vocal disapproval of Amos's superstitions. 'Where is it?' She cast a quick glance about her feet, fearful of stepping on the animal.

'Oh, I haven't actually seen it, but there's its basket.' The boy pointed to something under the bench seat that Jo had not noticed until now. A shallow wickerwork basket lined with a piece of warm blanket, and jammed securely into the only available alcove that presented itself. It made a cosy little nest, and she wondered where its owner was.

Perhaps the influx of two extra people aboard the *Kitti-wake* had been too much, and it had taken refuge elsewhere. Maybe with Amos?

'I can't see the *Sea Swallow*, can you?' she enquired, just as Dan rejoined them.

'He's fishing in the opposite direction.' The skipper's voice was curt.

'To make sure I don't cast a blight on his chances of a good catch, I expect.' Jo tried to speak lightly, but her voice came out flat, betraying the sudden bleakness that caught at her spirits. Perhaps Tessa had been right, and she should go back inland. She did not fit in among this sea-faring community, their ways and outlook were totally alien to anything she knew, and if Amos and Tessa were typical, she was not likely to be accepted among them even if she had been able to remain at the cottage.

'They're pulling in the net.' Dan's voice speaking to Chris, above a mechanical clatter, broke across her thoughts, and he strode away again. Interested despite herself, Jo pressed her nose to the window beside her brother and watched with fascination as the dark, bulging net was raised and swung dripping across the deck until it was over an erection of boards fixed in the centre, much like the fiddles Dan had slotted into the stove.

'Roddy says they untie the cod end of the net and drop the fish into the pound,' Chris informed her, proud of his newly acquired knowledge, and sure enough Lance reached up and untied the bottom end of the net as soon as it was swung over the cage made by the boards, and allowed the contents to spill safely within their confines. She saw Dan reach down over the boards and straighten up again, with a brown-backed, orange-spotted fish in his hand. A plaice for Hannah? It flipped feebly, and Jo suddenly felt sorry for the pile of gasping creatures, torn from their element to die in order to provide sustenance for others. For the first time she understood the feelings of confirmed vegetarians, and felt glad for the minute crabs and sundry small marine creatures that took immediate opportunity to quit the pile of flopping fish, and hasten to the rail where they dropped back overboard, unchallenged because they were too small to be of use.

'I wish I could go out there and help,' Chris said wistfully, and Jo shook her head.

'You mustn't. Dan said not.' She felt glad he had insisted on instant obedience from the boy. With the arrival of the net full of fish the scene on deck exploded into intense activity. Chris would only have been in the way, and what was worse might hinder the men and incur Dan's wrath. He had not wanted to bring them with him in the first place.

'Look at the gulls!' Chris shouted excitedly, his attention distracted by another wonder. Out of nowhere a cloud of squalling birds wheeled and dived about the boat in hungry anticipation. A knife blade caught the light and winked wickedly, and Lance and Dan settled to their task of gutting and cleaning their catch. Once or twice a gull, bolder than the others, dived on the mound to try and steal a fish, but invariably got distracted as one of the men, without bothering to look up, flicked some offal in its direction and it flew off, satisfied. Roddy had disappeared into the shallow hold, Jo could just see the top of his fiery head moving about above the level of the deck boards.

'Roddy boxes the fish.' Chris seemed to have learned a lot from his sojourn with the young lad, and Jo blessed Roddy's kindly interest. The multiplicity of new sights and sounds were providing a wonderful distraction for the child, and at least keeping one of them happy, she thought mournfully.

'Doesn't he want to take his turn working on deck?' It did not seem fair for the men to keep the freedom of the deck to themselves, while the boy worked alone in the cramped hold.

'Not Roddy,' Chris grinned. 'He reckons gutting's the coldest job in the world, particularly in a wind like this.' There was no doubt he was repeating the redhead's own words.

'So that's why Dan keeps him in the hold.' The skipper of the *Kittiwake* was a strange mixture, Jo mused, outwardly hard and unapproachable, but subject to unexpected flashes of kindness. It must be bitterly cold on deck. No wonder the men who worked there liked kye! A closer look at their arms, bared to the elbow, showed them to be as wet as the fish they handled.

'I'll make their kye.' She swung to her feet, and realised her legs had gone numb. She looked at her watch. 'I can't believe it!' she gasped. They had been at sea for several hours, that had fled like minutes with the interest they held. 'Where's the kettle?' She ignored the pins and needles in her feet and made her way to the urn for water.

'If you're making kye, that's no good.' Dan stuck his head inside the door. 'You'll have to make that in the dixie—just add the cocoa and plenty of sugar and a knob of butter. The water's already in it, ready to boil up.'

'Where do you keep your tin of cocoa?' She had to ask him; she hadn't seen one about, and she knew she had looked in all the cupboards there were in the small enclosure.

'It isn't in a tin, it's in slab form.' He reached down and picked up what Jo had taken to be a large bar of chocolate. 'I'll break it for you, it's hard.' It presented him with no trouble, his strong fingers snapped the slab into useable pieces which he dropped straight into the dixie as it stood. 'Boil it, but for goodness' sake don't let it boil over,' he warned her. 'Otherwise you can have the job of cleaning up the mess.' And he departed to resume his task beside Lance.

'He treats you as if you're a real part of the crew,' Chris commented enviously.

'That's not a privilege,' Jo snapped ungraciously. If she could, she thought mutinously, she would have liked to turn up the flame under the dixie of kye and walk out, and leave it to boil over at its leisure—and Dan to clear up the mess. The wide expanse of water surrounding the *Kittiwake* silently derided her wishful thinking, and she fumed in silence, keeping a careful eye on the dixie, since she had no illusions that Dan would carry out his threat, and refuse to let her ashore until she had cleared up any spills. Tiny though the boat's accommodation was, it was kept scrupulously clean, a pointer to the fastidious habits of its owner.

'You're not a bad galley hand,' Dan grinned as he tasted his drink, and cupped the enamel mug in both hands to unfreeze his fingers. Jo shuddered in sympathy as she watched the men hose down the deck when they finished cleaning the fish, and when they had stowed away the boards of the pound, hose themselves down as well. Even Roddy came in for the same treatment.

'I'd rather have him cold than dirty,' Dan responded to her protest, 'we'll all wash down in fresh water as soon as we're ashore, but there's an hour to go before then.' And a mug of hot liquid to drink, and one of Hannah's cookies to eat, with hands that he made sure were clean. Being obliged to approve his action made Jo more annoyed than ever.

'I can't see the shore.' Chris had his nose glued to the wheelhouse window again, the attraction of his surroundings even surmounting that of his cookie. 'I thought you said we should see the Claw Rocks coming in?'

'So we shall, but they're too far away just now, and the drizzle would blot them out anyway.' A faint splatter of wet on the window, that Jo had thought came from the hose, turned her towards Dan in sudden dismay.

'It's not going to be misty, is it? Or—or—anything?' Her expression betrayed her qualms. What if it got rough and she was sick? She put her untasted mug down on the stove with undignified haste.

'Of course not, there's too strong a wind blowing,' Dan scoffed. 'It gave you back the tea leaves just now, remember?' he laughed. 'And it'll be smoother going on the way back, we'll be riding the tide, so you can drink your kye. It won't make you sick, and it'll help to keep you warm.'

He read her thoughts with deflating accuracy, and his keen glance dared her to leave her drink, and she raised her mug defiantly to her lips. To her surprise the contents were good, more food than drink, and the heat of it seeped welcome fingers through her, relaxing her taut muscles, and she finished the mugful without any trouble.

'Come and stand by me up front; you'll see where we're going then. You won't feel quite so shut in.' How had he defined what she was feeling? Jo wondered, but the clearer windows up by the wheel gave an unobstructed view all round them, and she peered out, feeling happier.

'I'm turning her back home, now.' The engine shivered into life again after its steady, slow pulling of the last hour or so, but instead of butting into an oncoming sea, the *Kittiwake* rode on top of the long, slow rollers that bore it shorewards on the pull of the tide. It was a pleasant, soothing sensation, and Jo found she could keep her feet easily enough now, the smooth dips and rises presenting her with no difficulty. She did not even feel anxious when Roddy, with time on his hands again, collected Chris to show him the work he had done in the hold. Lance went with them, so he was there to check any over-abundance of enthusiasm, and Jo stood beside Dan at the wheel, content to enjoy the ride.

'Leave the dixie and the mugs,' he told her, 'I take those back to the house where there's plenty of hot water and soap.' So she left them, and remained with him, at peace for the moment, for with the urgency of the work gone, and the others out on deck, Dan's mood mellowed to match her own dreamy content, though his eyes remained alert, constantly searching his surroundings.

'Are you looking for the *Sea Swallow*?' A small cloud still hovered over her new-found peace.

'No, Amos has gone right out to the other side of the bay. He'll come into harbour from a different direction, probably he'll wait until nearly the turn of the tide.' He paused for a moment, his face serious, and then he said, 'Jo, you mustn't let Amos worry you.' He spoke as if he had been awaiting the opportunity to broach the subject. And now, when there was just the two of them together, was a propitious moment. 'His superstitions rule his life, but they can't be allowed to rule the lives of others,' he went on with quiet firmness. 'Even his own family see the sense of that. For a niece of his, Hannah isn't all that superstitious, really,' he smiled. 'And Roddy's his grandson, and he's as free thinking as any modern youngster.'

'Is everyone in St Mendoc related?' Jo asked lightly. The old fisherman's attitude had worried her, though she would not admit it, particularly to Dan.

'A lot of them belong to one family,' Dan replied. 'Years ago isolation and lack of transport encouraged intermarriage, but of course it's different now, easy travel's brought a breath of fresh air into the lives of the villagers. And into their thinking, though of course Amos's generation are too set in their ways to change over-much,' he acknowledged the inevitable without criticism. 'But the younger generation, ours and Roddy's, seek their partners where they choose,' he said. 'A different background can be an advantage,' he added, apropos of nothing. 'A rut's cosy, but it can be stifling too.'

Tessa was from a different background. A flower farm.

An attractive setting for a beautiful woman, Jo thought forlornly.

'Ah, there's another!' Dan stiffened suddenly, and his exclamation broke across her thoughts, forceful with an undercurrent of anger. He throttled the engine down to idling speed, and swiftly lashed the wheel. 'Stay where you are,' he bade her. 'I'll be back in a minute,' and then he was gone, striding away with a sense of urgency so strong that it communicated itself to Jo and left her tense. Forgetting her earlier resolution, she disobeyed him, and followed him outside.

'He's on the starboard side,' Lance called, already hanging over the rail watching something on the water below, and Jo felt her throat go dry. What was it Dan had stopped the boat for? Pieces of wreckage? A rowing boat, perhaps? She had not seen one, but she had not seen anything on the water besides themselves. Maybe it was a floating lifebelt, or—or—hurriedly she stopped her thoughts from going any further.

'Chris, come to me. Come here!' sharply, as the boy hesitated, and he slowly turned and dragged reluctant feet in her direction, wanting to go to the rail with Roddy instead.

'I want to watch,' he complained.

'You might be in the way. Wait for a minute or two.' It was a feeble excuse, but she dared not let him approach the rail. She was afraid of what he might see. For a child he had received shocks enough. Jo herself felt battered by the events of the last few months, and cringed from what might appear above the rail as Dan and Lance between them dropped a weighted hand net something like a hammock over the side of the boat, and did some trawling of their own. A tense moment passed and then Roddy called, 'It's in!' and the men started to pull the net up, slowly and carefully as if they did not want to upset whatever it was they had caught. Jo shut her eyes as the net emerged dripping into sight. It was cowardice, she knew, but she could not help it.

'Don't stand there looking scared—come and help!' Dan's voice, tinged with impatience, cut sharply through her horror, and she shivered and opened her eyes.

'What is it?' Chris asked curiously, and stepped away from his sister, snapping her back to instant life.

'Chris, come back!'

'Let him come, it's only a bird.' Once again Dan seemed to read her thoughts, and Jo found her eyes drawn downwards to the net, which he and Lance lowered on to the deck, and knelt beside it regardless of the risk of soaking their trousers in the process. As soon as they had swilled themselves down after dealing with the catch they changed from waders into ordinary rubber boots, and from above their knees they were no longer protected.

'It looks like a guillemot. Yes, it is.' His fingers explored the limp, slimy-looking mess that was all Jo could distinguish among the meshes.

'He's covered in waste oil.' Lance looked up at Jo briefly as he ran his hands under the net and raised it slightly to enable Dan to lift the bird with as little disturbance as possible. Even so it stirred, and the skipper nodded his satisfaction.

'There's a bit of life left in him, I think we might manage to save him. Roddy?' But Roddy had gone, and was already struggling back through the wheelhouse door with the wicker basket in his hands that Jo thought was there for a kitten.

'Warm some water, will you, Jo?' Dan called over his shoulder. 'Not too hot, I want it for a hot water bottle for this poor little creature.'

She sped to do his bidding, grateful for the steadier deck that enabled her to keep her feet while she worked. The guillemot, barely recognisable as a bird, with its feathers plastered to its body with the thick black oil, was another piece of the flotasm and jetsam Tessa said Dan collected. Just as much a piece as herself and Chris.

'We thought the basket was for a kitten.' Chris trotted close behind Dan, getting under his feet in his eagerness to help.

'You go into the wheelhouse in front of me, and take one end of the basket.' The skipper considerately let the boy hold the basket when he could have managed for himself far better. Jo hastily thrust her toe against the wheelhouse door to hold it open, sympathetic with his struggle to elbow his way through and give the child a clear passage at the same time. 'Wedge the basket into the alcove under the seat, it'll ride steady enough there.' Dan went on his knees to lift it in without disturbing the limp creature inside.

'Here's the hot water bottle.' Jo held it down to him, finding herself as keen to help as her brother.

'Thanks.' He reached up and behind him without looking up, and took the rubber hot water bottle from her hands. For a second he held it against his cheek, not trusting her to know enough not to make it too hot, she thought, and she stepped back, feeling rebuffed. 'He'll do now until we get home.'

'How will you clean him?' It looked a hopeless task. 'Surely it would be better to put the poor thing out of its misery?' she cried, distressed by her closer view of the half dead bird. 'It's cruel to try and keep it alive.' Indignation rose and blocked her speech, that Dan should contemplate prolonging the guillemot's suffering.

'You'll see the difference in him in a day or two,' he replied, unmoved by her tone. 'If you want to go outside with Lance and Roddy, Chris, keep a lookout in case there are any more birds that have been caught in the same oil slick, will you?' He smiled as the child hastened off. 'You haven't seen the pens at the back of Penderick House, then?' He glanced at her disturbed face and compressed lips as he unlashed the wheel and set the boat in motion again.

'What pens?' She felt angry with him for trying to change the subject.

'The pens for the seabirds I bring home with me,' he explained patiently, as if he might be talking to a recalcitrant child. 'The victims of the oil slicks,' he enlarged, seeing that he had gained her reluctant attention. 'Every trip we make we keep a lookout for them. All the ships in our fleet have instructions to do the same. Not that they need them,' he added thankfully, 'all our men would stop and pick up the birds anyway. They bring them straight up to the house when they find any. Some we can't save,' he added regretfully, 'but a lot of them we do, and after a week or two, when they're recovered, we're able to set them free again. At least it's something to counteract the tremendous losses caused by spilt oil.'

'Flotsam and jetsam,' Jo murmured.

'What?' His attention was only half on what she said, the rest of it on his task of swinging the boat on to its previous course towards the distant harbour.

'Oh, never mind.' Jo did not want to explain. It would mean telling him what Tessa had said, and admitting that the other girl's sneer had upset her. Instead she turned her head, and watched Dan's face. She could safely do that now, his eyes were intent on looking ahead, his head turned slightly away from her so that his features showed in sharp profile against the wheelhouse window. It was a strong face, the face of a man who knew where he was going, and who was accustomed to overcoming obstacles. The face of a man who could be gentle, too; now and again an inner core of compassion showed through, which under normal circumstances he hid pretty effectively under a tough outer shell. Children and animals, including birds, must be his Achilles heel. Compassion for Chris made him take her into his home—Jo did not delude herself that it was out of consideration for herself that he had taken them into Penderick House; his attitude to most grown-ups seemed to be one of impatient tolerance rather than liking.

'You can help me bring this little chap back to life when we get home if you like,' he told her, 'you'll see then how soon he'll respond. If he's going to, that is,' he added quietly.

'I'd like that.' She would dearly love to help bring the guillemot back to life, though the thought of doing it with Dan stirred her heart to a life she did not wish to have. With an effort she controlled her thoughts. If she helped Dan with his birds, it would be one way of repaying the Pendericks for their hospitality to herself and Chris, she told herself determinedly. She did not dare to offer them money for their keep. The thought had occurred to her, pride rejected the idea of accepting their board without payment of some kind, but she blanched at the thought of what Dan's reaction would be if she offered money. Offering her help would be an ideal way out. She felt happier now she had found a solution to at least this one problem.

'There's the Claw Rocks, coming up on our port side. Er—your left-hand side,' Dan elucidated with a grin as Jo swivelled her eyes this way and that, seeking vain direction.

'Then why didn't you say so?' she snapped, smarting once again under her own ignorance of all things nautical.

'Didn't think,' he retorted, unabashed, and met her glare with an amused look. 'We're not used to having landlubbers aboard the *Kittiwake*.' He made it into a taunt, and she gritted her teeth.

'I said the rocks looked worse from the sea.' His amusement faded, and he gestured ahead, and Jo forgot her vexation as she followed his signal, and met the visual impact of the cruel string of rocks, which drove every other thought from her head.

'Do you have to pass—those,' she gulped, 'every time you go out and come back?' Her heart turned over at the thought of the danger.

'If we come back on this side of the harbour, yes. It's the quickest way from where we've been today,' he told her practically.

'They're—horrible.' Even now, in calm weather, they exuded a menace that could be felt. The slight drizzle had stopped, and the sky lightened, but it still remained grey, and in the dull light the spear-shaped rocks stood black and grim out of the waste of water around them like some great beast of prey waiting silently, with awful patience, to claim its victim.

'There's no danger under normal circumstances.' Dan glanced down keenly at her face, which mirrored her feelings without need of words. 'It's only when there's a storm, or perhaps a boat drifting out of control with an engine breakdown, or maybe the steering mechanism fouled, or something.' He spoke lightly, trying to wipe away the dread that showed clear in her eyes. 'Look, the sun's coming out.' He distracted her attention, pointing beyond the Claw Rocks to where a thin shaft of sunlight found its way through the lowering clouds, and cut a swathe of light across the distant cliffs. It lit up a square of bright gold, and instinctively Jo stood on tiptoe to see better.

'That won't help,' he teased her shorter stature. 'We're still a good way off,' he reminded her.

'What is it?' It glinted like a bright penny among the vast expanse of dun-coloured cliff.

'It's a field at one of the flower farms.'

'Tessa's?' Somehow it did not seem so bright, now.

'No, the Tremaynes' holding is in the opposite direction. The farm where that field isn't has been worked for several years now, the people left and the place became derelict. That's why you can see the daffodils, they've been left to bloom on their own. In a flower farm that's being worked they're picked in tight bud, you never see a field of them in full colour like that.'

She should have known that, too. Tessa would have done. For the umpteenth time she felt at a disadvantage with the other girl, and smarted under the gall of it. Dan seemed to enjoy rubbing it in, too, which made it worse. Almost, she felt glad when they rounded the rim of the bay, and the arms of the harbour jutted out in welcome just ahead. Almost, but not quite. The brief hours she had spent with Dan in an environment that was wholly his own had given her a new insight into the character of the man behind the stern outer shell, a glimpse that she found enlightening, and wholly disturbing. The touch of his hand as he took the hot water bottle from her to tend the guillemot; his quick kiss, that for him was a moment's amusement, but for Jo it meant the closing of one book and the opening of another, totally different one, as yet unwritten, and who knew what words might be blazoned across its still virgin pages? Whose names linked, before the close of the final chapter . . .

'Dan! Cooee!' A tiny figure waved from the end of the harbour wall. A figure with fluttering skirts and long hair, that even from this distance Jo could see was dark, as Dan took the *Kittiwake* in a wide sweep to give him a straight run in through the harbour entrance, that from far off looked impossibly small to take the boat, but got wider by the minute as they approached, and with easy skill Dan pointed the vessel in and brought it to rest at the bottom of the stone steps in the exact spot from which they had set out earlier.

'Looking for fish again, Tessa?' Lance called up to the girl as he and Roddy jumped ashore and tied up. 'Isn't Amos back yet?'

'No, and anyway I had some from Amos yesterday,' she called back. 'I thought I'd try yours today.' Tessa swung her basket and smiled invitingly, making a pretty display of holding down her skirts against the playful wind that lifted them enough to show a pair of attractive, nylon-clad legs, and an underskirt of lacy frills that was as provocatively lovely as the girl herself, and essentially feminine. Jo felt suddenly scruffy in her warmly practical slacks and jersey.

'You'll grow fins if you eat so much fish,' Dan teased from the deck.

'I just fancied some for supper again tonight,' Tessa pouted prettily.

'Then you'd better take this one, I know it'll be good.' Dan dived into the hold and came out with a plastic container, and Jo caught sight of a brown body with bright spots on it.

'I thought you'd saved the plaice for Hannah?'

She should not have said it. It was none of her business, and Tessa threw her a look that told her so.

'Hannah won't mind,' she said indifferently, 'we've got an arrangement between us. Dan knows.' She threw the information at Jo with seeming carelessness, her casual manner hiding her barbed intention, but Jo did not miss, as Tessa intended she should not, the intimation of her close relationship with the family at Penderick House, that was deliberately designed to make Jo feel an outsider—an unwanted outsider.

'Tessa keeps Hannah supplied with flowers, and we keep her supplied with fish,' Dan smiled. 'Tessa suggested it, and it works very well.'

Tessa would suggest it, Jo thought caustically. It would provide the ideal excuse for her to visit Penderick House, and also a reason to be at the harbour to meet Dan's boat as it came in on the tide each day. She was dressed to impress rather than to keep herself warm; her toeless, high-heeled shoes were most unsuitable for walking the harbour wall, and Dan noticed them. He was observant enough where Tessa was concerned, thought Jo waspishly.

'Don't come down, the steps are wet and you'll spoil your

shoes.' He took the container of fish and vaulted easily over the rail on to the flight of steps. 'See Jo up the steps, will you, Lance,' he called over his shoulder, 'and Roddy, make sure Chris doesn't slip, the stones are a bit wet.' He was as considerate of the child as ever. He took the steps easily himself, two at a time, having disposed of the responsibility of his passengers, and even forgetting the guillemot in his eagerness to be with Tessa. Jo could forgive him for forgetting herself, but not the guillemot ... She raised her head to remind him of it, then changed her mind. It wouldn't be any use if she did tell him, any more than it had been reminding him that the plaice was for Hannah. She might have been mistaken in that, of course. Dan could have saved the fish for Tessa, knowing she would be there to meet him when they docked.

Jo wished heartily she had not come out on the trip at all. All the pleasure she had gained from it vanished, and only depression remained. The question mark hovering over the eventual fate of the seabird hung over her own too, in a different way. She pulled her mac about her, shrinking from the keen wind that seemed to cut more cruelly as they neared the top of the flight of steps, where Dan and Tessa stood, talking and laughing, absorbed in one another to the exclusion of all else.

'Here's your basket,' he smiled, and gave it back to the girl with the container of fish inside. 'Mind you cook the plaice properly,' he told her, mock serious, 'I prepared it specially for you.'

So it had been for Tessa, and not for Hannah. Jo's gloom deepened.

'You liked the way I cooked it the last time you came for a meal.' Tessa looked up at him, her black eyes laughing. 'Come and try it again some time,' she invited, 'I've found a new recipe.'

It sounded as if he went to the Tremaynes for a meal

fairly frequently. And no doubt he was a welcome visitor. Jo hovered miserably on the outskirts of the little group, wishing she could go and leave them, and contrarily glad that she could not, since it would leave Tessa victor on her own ground.

'I'll be off,' the other girl said surprisingly. 'Here's your lorry coming.' The rumble of an approaching engine warned of its arrival, and the group broke up. Roddy and Dan returned to the deck, but not before Tessa stood on tiptoe suddenly, and kissed the tip of the skipper's chin.

'That's for the fish,' she laughed, her amusement tinkling across the harbour as Dan offered hastily, 'For another like that you can have the whole catch.' 'Some other time,' she returned softly, 'when we're more private.' She threw a mocking look at Jo and swung away, waving gaily to the driver of the lorry as they passed.

'I'll leave the unloading to you tonight, Alf,' Dan called as the man drew to a halt and jumped down from his machine.

'That's O.K. by me, Skipper. I'll cope and then I can give young Roddy here a lift home. What about the young 'un?' He noticed Chris for the first time. 'Has't got a new apprentice?' he asked seriously.

'Aye, and he's shaping well.' Dan ducked back out of the wheelhouse with the basket under his arm.

He hasn't forgotten the guillemot after all! A wave of relief passed through Jo, and she became conscious of Chris's excited chatter, bubbling over with delight at the fisherman's teasing and Dan's praise.

'I'll take the mugs and the dixie back home. Thanks for coping, Alf,' Lance added, and lent another pair of hands to relieve Dan's burden. The lorry driver grinned.

' 'Twon't take long before we have that lot in tins,' he declared, and with a friendly nod towards Jo he joined Roddy on the *Kittiwake*'s deck.

'Tessa's gone.' Dan looked round as if he expected to find her waiting near where they parked the car.

'She wouldn't have gone if she'd known you weren't going to stay and unload the catch,' Lance predicted, with an impish grin in Jo's direction that tilted her own lips upwards. This time, it seemed to be Tessa who was worsted, she thought gleefully, and felt her satisfaction in the thought dimmed because the other girl was not aware of it too.

And I didn't even get the chance to tell her I wasn't seasick, either, she mourned silently. Perhaps after all it was Tessa who had scored again, and not herself.

CHAPTER SIX

'THAT was the factory, with the figures for the catch—yours and Amos's.' Julian returned from the telephone and picked up his after-dinner coffee. 'You both had a good haul.' He settled himself back in his armchair with every appearance of relief.

'Which had the biggest?' Chris piped up interestedly, and Julian smiled.

'The *Kittiwake*, of course,' he teased.

'So I didn't cast a blight on the fishing after all,' Jo observed, and try as she might she could not keep the bite out of her voice.

'I told you not to let Amos worry you,' Dan said sharply, and turned from helping himself to more coffee. 'I said . . .'

'Oh, never mind Amos, tell us how much we've earned,' Lance cut impatiently across the suddenly brittle atmosphere.

'Earned?' Chris looked up puzzled from his seat on the rug.

'Yes, earned,' Lance emphasised. 'You don't think we go out cleaning and boxing fish in a freezing wind, for fun, do you?' he sounded scandalised, and drew a laugh from the others which blew away the last of the tension. 'The *Kittiwake*'s a working boat, my lad, not a pleasure steamer,' he rubbed his point home. 'The canning factory has to be kept supplied with fish, or the people it employs would have no work to do.'

'Here's the factory tally.' Julian handed Lance the slip of paper on which he had taken down the telephone mes-

sage and his brother glanced at it and nodded, as if satisfied, before handing it on to Dan.

'Mmm, we've earned our keep, and the *Kittiwake* a new
bit for her engine.' Dan folded the paper and slipped it into
the inside pocket of his jacket.

'But how do you know?' Chris persisted, clearly intent
on learning all about this fascinating new trade, and Dan
responded with the patience he invariably showed towards
the boy.

'Each man on the crew has a share,' he explained, 'and
the boat itself is counted as another share, to pay for the
fuel and the upkeep. Your share,' he took out the slip of
paper again and studied it seriously, 'your share comes to a
pound,' he said gravely, and the boy's eyes widened.

'My share?'

'I took you on as a crew member for the day,' Dan reminded him.

'No, Dan! I can't allow ...'

'I don't accept voluntary labour from anyone.' Dan met
Jo's indignant glare across the boy's head.

'Does that include mine?' If he offers me money, I'll
throw it back at him, thought Jo furiously. How dared he
patronise them like this? They were under his roof as involuntary guests, not beggars. All her pride rose in protest
at the idea of accepting Dan's money as well as his hospitality.

'I don't take on women as crew members.' He sugared
his coffee and stirred it unhurriedly, blandly unmoved by
her anger. 'If a passenger volunteers to make a hot drink for
the crew, we accept their help with gratitude.' His blue eyes
glinted into hers, challenging her to remind him that he had
called her a galley hand, and she bit her lip, compelling
herself to silence. If she flung the reminder at him, as it was
on the tip of her tongue to do, he would pay her as a crew

member, and that her pride would not allow. And Dan knew it ...

'A whole pound!' Chris had the dazed look of a treasure hunter who has just come across a golden hoard. 'It'll buy me a new bird book,' he gloated.

'And a sketching pad and pencil, if you want it,' Dan encouraged him, and Jo fumed in helpless silence. Dan knew Chris wanted another bird book, to replace the one they had had to leave behind in the cottage. And once again he had driven her into a corner, knowing she would not disappoint the child by refusing to let him accept the money. 'There's rather a nice shop in the village which sells books and artists' materials in the tourist season,' Dan waxed informative, being deliberately aggravating, thought Jo vexedly, but she could see no way to stop him without spoiling Chris's pleasure. 'They've probably got their new season's stock in by now, why not come into St Mendoc with me tomorrow? I've got to go and see about a spare part for the *Kittiwake*'s engine, you can come with me if you like and see if they've got what you want.'

'Is it a big job, on your engine?' Julian asked lazily, smiling at the boy's excited acceptance.

'No, it's stuttering a bit, that's all. I can manage her until I've got a replacement part, I know how to nurse her along,' Dan said complacently.

Trust Dan to be sure of his ability to cope! Jo thought waspishly. One half of her loved his rugged self-confidence, the other, angry half of her longed to put a dent in his arrogance, and did not know how.

'You and your boat!' Julian laughed indulgently. 'But I heard Hannah say she wanted to go into St Mendoc for some groceries or something. She might like a lift too,' he put in a word for the housekeeper.

'That gives me two passengers,' Dan agreed good-humouredly. 'How about you, Jo?' He raised his eyebrows quizzically in her direction. 'Do you want to go into St Mendoc for anything?'

'I want to go to look for rooms for myself and Chris,' she snapped ungraciously.

'I was rather hoping you'd agree to stay with us for a while, until the insurance on the cottage is settled.' Julian turned towards her, his usual gentle manner troubled. 'I've been in contact with the solicitors today, and they've got everything in hand, but you know these things take a little time to settle, and I may need you to sign things and so on,' he explained. 'I'm afraid my leg doesn't take kindly to the streets of St Mendoc these days,' he added ruefully, 'to say the least of it they're steep, and I find the cobbles difficult to negotiate, particularly if they're wet.' He got up from his chair to replenish his coffee cup at the tray, and his limp was more pronounced, as it usually was at the end of the day, when he was tired.

'I would come to see you,' Jo protested. 'There'd be no need for you to bother coming out to St Mendoc, all you would need to do is phone, and I'd come straight away.' It was good of Julian to see to the insurance on the cottage for her, it was unthinkable that he should be put to more inconvenience than was necessary.

'The cottages in St Mendoc don't usually boast telephones,' Dan cut across her protest drily. 'The hotel does, but that's to be expected in one with a four-star rating.' He gave her oblique warning of the possible cost of accommodation there. 'I'm afraid you'll have to put up with us for a little while longer.' His eyes mocked her across the width of the hearth, and even when she closed her own in the welcome dark of her bedroom later she could not shut them out, so that long after the rest of the house slumbered, she tossed restlessly, and at last got up and drew the curtains, to watch the string of lights far out to sea where part of the Penderick fleet hunted, silent and intent, gleaning the dark waters.

'I'm going to have a look at the guillemot before break-fast, if you'd like to come with me?' Dan met her on the way downstairs the next morning. 'You're up early,' he commented, his eyes keen on her face.

'I thought I'd go for a walk before breakfast, it's a nice morning.' She did not care if it was pouring with rain so long as she could escape from her room, which felt like a prison after her sleepless night

'Do you think the bird will still be alive?' She hesitated. She felt depressed already, and if ...

'I'm pretty certain he will be. Come,' Dan took her elbow persuasively, 'you saw how he perked up when you helped me to clean the oil off him before dinner last night.'

It was incredible. Jo didn't believe that the limp, oily creature lying helplessly in Dan's cupped palms, while under his direction she gently brushed the oil soaked feathers with warm soapy water, could even want to live, so weak it seemed. The hopelessness of their task choked her, the tears rolled unchecked down her cheeks at the pitiful waste, blinding her eyes so that she rubbed them with her sleeve to clear her vision—her hands were too soapy to reach for her handkerchief.

'I wouldn't have let you help me if I thought it would make you cry. No, let the bird rest for a while.' Dan laid it down and took both her hands in his own, his face creased with concern.

'I'm not usually so silly.'

'You've gone through a bad time lately.' Without re-leasing her he turned and picked up a clean towel that waited in readiness to dry out the guillemot's feathers. 'Let me dry your hands, you're all soapy. There, you can dry your eyes with your hanky now. Let me do it,' as she fumbled, still unable to see properly. 'That's better.' With tender hands he dried her cheeks. 'Brown eyes are made for smiles, not tears,' he admonished her. Was it really Dan who whispered to her? Words that sounded like poetry to her ears as he drew her to him, his head bent above her in a concerned manner that had more of Julian in it than the bluff owner of the *Kittiwake*.

'Cry away,' he urged, and gathered her close in his arms, as if she was a child in need of comfort. 'In a storm, you either bend or break.'

'I daren't let go in front of Chris.' Her words were muffled against his chest, her face turned down so that she need not look into his. If only he would, he could give her all the strength her heart yearned for, and it need never stand on its own again.

'You can let go in front of me.' Dan pressed her to him, and his words stabbed her heart like a knife. It mattered if she let go in front of Chris. Because of her brother's affection, her distress would upset him too. It would not upset Dan unduly, because he did not care for her, except for a humane concern that seemed a part of the man for all his fellow creatures.

She raised her head, leaning away from him, and found his face hovering close above her hair, as if—she tensed, and caught her breath. His last kiss had been a taunt. She did not want another out of pity.

Unk!

'There, what did I tell you?' A slow smile wiped the concern from Dan's face, and he gestured down towards their feet. 'Look, he's feeling better already.'

'Was that the guillemot?' Her own distress temporarily forgotten, Jo stared at the bird. Two shoe-button eyes looked unwinkingly back.

'Help me to shower him off,' Dan urged her, 'then we'll feed him if we can.'

This time Jo cradled the bird, while Dan used a bathroom hair spray to swill its feathers free of soap.

'He'll have to have another wash either tomorrow or the next day, depending on how he progresses.'

'He seems to be enjoying it.' Jo watched in amazement as the bird tried feebly to ruffle its feathers under the tepid shower.

'They usually do,' Dan grinned. 'In fact the ones that are in the convalescent pens will try and wriggle under the shower for a free bath if you leave it on. Now let's blot the drips off him and see if he'll take a strip of fish.' He rolled the bird and Jo's hands all together inside the warm towel. 'You can loose him, now.' She drew her hands away reluctantly, conscious of the strong support of Dan's fingers. Longing for them to stay there, and too proud to let hers lie within their clasp. She watched as he patted the guillemot's wet body as it lay with its head outside the towel, blinking contentedly, as if it knew it had reached a safe haven at last.

'Now let's try him with a strip of fish.' Dan picked up a long, raw sliver and dangled it enticingly over the bird's head. For a second or two nothing happened, and then with a quick dart its beak clasped on the fish, and with a shake of the feathered head it disappeared down its throat.

'He'll do for tonight.' After another piece of fish had been swallowed, and a third refused, Dan returned the bird to its basket.

'Do you want another hot water bottle for it?'

'No, I keep lamps over the sick ones, similar to incubators in a chicken hatchery. It keeps a gentle warmth in the pens, which is enough until they're on their feet again.' He shut the pen door behind him. 'I'll show you the others tomorrow,' he promised, 'it's too near dinner time to visit them now.' He would show her what work he wanted her to do, Jo guessed, but she made no comment. It seemed the only way of relieving her of her obligation to him, and she accompanied him in to dinner in silence.

Now, in the fresh, clean light of a new day, unaccountably she shrank from facing what she had helped him to do last night.

'He's not here.' She tensed, waiting for Dan to open the pen door, and found she was trembling.

Unk!

'He's waiting at the door for some more fish. It didn't take him long to learn,' Dan laughed.

'His feathers look a different colour this morning. Oh, just look at the size of his feet!' Jo let out a gusty laugh of sheer relief.

'They'd be a big ache if he had to walk instead of fly,' Dan grinned. 'Let's see if he's prepared to be friendly.' He closed the pen door behind them and bent his knees beside the guillemot, upright now and watching them both hopefully.

'Most of them like their chins scratched.' He put out a tentative forefinger.

'Birds don't have chins,' Jo giggled, gay with relief from her previous strain.

'Well, the feathered equivalent, then,' Dan conceded loftily. 'Look, he likes it.' To Jo's surprise the bird lifted its head with every appearance of enjoyment, and sat perfectly still while Dan ruffled its throat feathers.

'Here's your reward.' The man held out a piece of fish, and this time the guillemot did not hesitate. With a quick gulp and a headshake it disappeared.

Unk!

'Does that mean thank you, or I want some more, I wonder?' Jo chuckled, and at the sound of her voice the bird shuffled hopefully towards her. 'Let's call him Flippers.' She raised a delighted face towards her companion.

'No!' Dan said sternly, and he put his hand under her arm and drew her to her feet. 'The birds become very friendly, particularly the guillemots.'

'Then why...?' Puzzled and rebuffed, she stared at him in open surprise.

'Because you have to learn to let them go, and giving them a name simply makes it more difficult.' Dan led her firmly outside the cage and shut the door with equal firmness on the bird, which plodded hopefully behind them. 'It isn't fair to the birds to try and chain them,' he said quietly.

'I wasn't thinking of chaining him...'

'Affection can be just as strong a chain as one forged from iron. It isn't kind to make a pet out of a wild creature, they're best among their own kind, leading their natural lives. Come and look at the birds in this pen,' he propelled her insistently away from the disappointed Unk! which followed their departure. 'In another few days, this lot can be set free if they continue to float as they're doing now.' He gestured towards a group of assorted seabirds disporting themselves in an artificial pool inside the second netting enclosure.

'Why shouldn't they float? They're water birds.'

'The cleaning process can take some of the natural oil from their feathers. I have to make sure they're capable of remaining on top of the water before I let them go,' Dan explained. 'It's quite a sight to see them take off,' he added enthusiastically, 'you'll have to come with me when we set this lot free, I usually take them to the tip of Penderick Head and set them loose from there.'

Freedom meant a great deal to her companion, Jo surmised. 'Affection can be just as strong a chain as one forged from iron ...' There spoke a loner, one whose feet loved the feel of a shifting deck, and the fierce challenge of the elements to pit his strength against. It would need a strong woman to win this man, a strong woman to hold him. Tessa maybe had this strength. Did she herself? Jo wondered. Or did Dan regard her inexperience of his alien world as weakness on her part, an object of scorn, to laugh about when he was in Tessa's company?

'It wasn't today I wanted to get the groceries, Mr Julian, it was tomorrow,' Hannah told him reproachfully as she cleared away the breakfast things. 'The shops will all be shut today. Your bookshop as well,' she told Chris.

'And I happen to know your engine bit won't be ready for you, the foreman at the boatyard told me to give you a message when I took our day's consignment to the flower train this morning. He won't have it in until tomorrow,' a light voice informed Dan from the doorway, and Jo's heart sank.

Tessa! Everywhere she went, she seemed to bump into the girl.

'I've brought you some narcissus, Hannah.' Tessa turned with an ingratiating smile to the housekeeper. 'They're my favourite perfume. I think you remember people by their favourite perfume.' She glanced provocatively across at Dan.

So even when she left the house Tessa intended to leave a reminder of herself behind. The girl fought her battles with all the cunning of a military tactician, and in spite of her dislike, Jo had to admire her determination. Tessa wanted Dan Penderick, and she meant to have him, even if Dan was not aware of the fact. Jo wondered if he was really blind to the girl's persistent campaign. He was certianly not blind to her beauty, that much was evident when he had let her kiss him in return for the fish when the *Kittiwake* docked. It was a reversal of roles, for the hunter to become the quarry, Jo thought without humour, and wondered if Dan minded. He was of the type to do his own hunting, savouring the chase as well as the capture. With Tessa, maybe he did not mind. Jo considered her dispassionately. She was startlingly beautiful, with a wild, gypsy loveliness that would make lesser hearts than Dan's beat faster. Jo felt her own delicate loveliness pale into insignificance beside Tessa.

'Can Melanie come out to play?' Deprived of his looked-forward-to outing, Chris sought an alternative.

'Melanie can stay and do the chores for a change,' Tessa snapped. 'And I'll have a morning free for once. You've got nothing to do, either, now you can't get your engine part.' Her voice was soft, inviting, and she spoke to Dan alone.

'I've got one or two things to see to.' He smiled back at her, his blue eyes teasing.

'I'll stay and help you,' she said promptly.

'To bait lobster pots?'

'Ugh!' Tessa shook her head firmly. Obviously the task did not appeal to her.

'Go and tend your flowers.' His smile softened. 'What I'm about to do is no job for a pretty girl.'

He hadn't minded Jo helping him clean the guillemot free from oil. He did not seem to think that was not a job for her. Maybe he expected her—Jo—to help him with the lobster pots. To circumvent such a possibility she immediately made up her mind on another outing for herself and Chris.

'We'll go along the beach and look for stones. You never know, we might find some I can make into a bracelet to match Melanie's pendant.'

She did not think Tessa would refuse to let the young girl accept it. Certainly she would not say anything in front of Dan, and thus confident of going unchallenged, Jo walked past Tessa with her chin held high, taking a willing Chris, who was keen to help find a present for his new friend.

'What d'you bait lobster pots with?' he wanted to know, and Jo shook her head. She did not care, and had no intention of asking, particularly in front of Tessa.

'Fish offal.' Lance saved her the trouble as he shrugged into a windcheater and made for his car. 'Why, do you want to help?' he enquired with a grin.

'No, thanks!' No wonder Tessa refused. For once Jo felt some sympathy for her rival, and then wondered what had made her think of the other girl as that. Rivalry meant competition, and Jo had no intention of competing for Dan or any other man. Her dignity rose at the thought of regarding him—any man—as a prize to be won.

'We can reach the beach by the creek path.' She collected their own macs and slipped out of the side door, half running on to the soft grass, and down the slope where the daffodils grew so that she should not bump into Tessa and Dan. She slowed down as soon as her feet found the path beside the creek. It had become a favourite walk with her since they came to stay at Penderick House, the quiet green banks providing a haven of peace to her storm-battered spirit, that came to St Mendoc to find rest, and found Dan instead. And a whirlwind of emotion that caught her in its vortex, a helpless victim without power or will to free herself. Dan stood calmly at the eye of the storm, untouched by its fury, remaining aloof and as indifferent to her as he seemed to be to anything except his boat, she thought angrily.

'Let's look for crabs as well.' Chris skipped along by her side in a manner that did her heart good. He was no longer conscious of every step he took because walking no longer hurt.

'That's a good idea.' Jo welcomed his suggestion, since the tide was well out and the rock pools would be a good distance away from the foot of the cliffs. Now her eyes had been opened to the danger, she could see a dozen places where small rock slides had occurred along the shore.

'There's a crab in this one, but he's too small.' Chris slid off the upthrust of rocks back on to the sand, and cast around for another pool.

'Don't go near the foot of the cliffs,' Jo warned.

'Don't worry, I won't,' her brother retorted. The loss of their cottage and the pitiful evidence of its one-time garden in crumbs on the beach had frightened the child into caution as well. 'There's a bigger pool down by the break-water. Perhaps it'll be warm enough to paddle.' He set off, and Jo stopped by the rock pool he had just deserted, inquisitive to see the crab that was too small. With Chris's departure the silence on the beach became absolute, except for a rhythmic squeaking sound that probably came from an insecure board on the breakwater. She sat down on a piece of the rock top that was worn flat by the action of the tides, and bent over the mirror-like surface of the trapped water. Only another tide would release it, and the tiny marine creatures it contained. The crab was there, and one or two unidentified forms of life that scuttled for shelter as she bent her face close above them. The slight disturbance caused by their flight sent a miniature ripple wavering across the surface, shaking her own reflection momentarily out of recognition, and then the crystal clear pool steadied again and her own winsome loveliness gazed back at her, in company with another, stronger, suntanned face topped by a shock of black hair, and a pair of blue eyes that gazed laughingly straight into her own.

'You're admiring your own reflection in the water,' Dan accused her. 'Remember what happened to Narcissus, and beware!'

'I'm doing nothing of the sort.' Startled, she turned hastily, and almost lost her balance.

'Careful, it isn't very deep, but it's big enough to wet you if you fall in.' He put out his hand and steadied her, and she jumped to her feet, scarlet with mortification. Why did she always have to behave in this clumsy fashion when Dan was with her? she wondered, furious with herself. Once again she had made herself an object of derision, and she looked round hastily, half expecting to see Tessa with Dan.

'If you're looking for Chris, he's safe enough down by the breakwater,' Dan misinterpreted her seeking glance.

'You startled me. I didn't hear you come.'

'The rowlocks made enough noise to warn you,' he protested. 'They creaked like a banshee.'

'Creaked? I thought that was a loose board on the breakwater.'

'There's no tide in to move the boards,' he pointed out, 'and not enough wind either.'

Her own ignorance had let her down again. Jo smarted under his amused smile. Tessa would have recognised the sound, it would have been as familiar to her as the ring of bicycle bells had been to Jo in the university town where she lived for so long.

'I thought you were baiting lobster pots.' She threw it at him like a challenge, her poise shaken by his unexpected appearance, when she thought she and Chris had the beach to themselves.

'Er—not exactly baiting them.' To Jo's astonishment, Dan looked faintly embarrassed. 'Just checking to see if the pots have caught anything, that's all.'

He *had* said he was baiting them. She remembered his words quite distinctly, they had prompted Chris's question to Lance, so she could not be mistaken. He had lied to Tessa. Why? A sudden thought struck her. Perhaps Dan was as reluctant for herself and Tessa to be in one another's company as Jo was herself. Maybe he found her continued presence at Penderick House difficult to explain away to the dark-haired girl. Tessa would be unlikely to look kindly on the presence of a possible rival on what she seemed to regard as her own territory. So why had Dan backed up Julian, when he suggested she stay on at the house? Probably for Julian's sake. Dan had a strong regard for his family and his home that even his love for the *Kittiwake* could not outweigh.

'Will you take the lobsters back with you, if you find any?' Chris joined them; Dan was like a magnet to the boy, Jo thought, and the man seemed in no way averse to the child's company, in fact he encouraged his persistent questions.

'Yes, I'll take any that are there. You can come with me if you like,' he offered.

'Ooh, please! Are you coming too, Jo?'

'No, I'm going to look for stones, like I said.' Dan had not asked her. He did not ask her now, even out of politeness after what Chris had said, and Jo's proud spirit shrank into herself rather than ask to go with them. She would go for a walk by herself. Dan need not be afraid she would foist her company on him, and perhaps embarrass him in front of Tessa.

With a perfunctory wave she turned her back on the departing rowboat, hearing the creak of its rowlocks like derisive laughter behind her. There was a path up the cliffs from the beach. She disdained to walk along the sands any further, the stones for Melanie's bracelet would have to wait. If Dan intended to check his lobster pots close to the shore she would be under his surveillance the whole of the time she was on the sands, and the idea did not appeal to her.

The cliff path was steep and she paused for breath as the sun came out with sudden warmth, forerunner of the soft air that would soon star the lanes with primroses. With urgent longing, she wished the summer would come, wished the dark winter well behind her, with its troubles and its problems safely solved. Her eyes followed the sunlight where it lit up the brooding cliffs, and caught the field of daffodils that had shown up so clearly from the deck of the *Kittiwake* the day before.

'I'll go and have a look at it,' Jo decided. It would give a point to her walk, and a reason if Dan questioned why she had quit the beach instead of remaining there to look for stones as she originally intended. With renewed energy she started to climb again. Now and then she caught sight of

Dan and her brother in the rowing boat far below, and some way behind her. They appeared to have stopped, probably to check one of the lobster pots, and firmly dismissing the fisherman from her mind Jo gained the soft turf on the cliff top with a puff of relief.

The view was superb across wild, rolling countryside, that in the sunshine lost its bleak look and took on a majesty that caught and held her. She could learn to love this alien countryside as much as she had learned to love one of its sons. The automatic light from the end of Penderick Head winked in a friendly fashion as she turned her back on the fitful wind to get her breath a moment, and she stared at it, a sharp pain in her heart. The light must mean home, to Dan, coming in from the fishing grounds. A welcoming warmth reaching out through storm and wind to draw him back to harbour. He did not need to fish, she knew that from Hannah. Any more than Lance needed to, or Julian to look after the canning factory, but she admired the spirit that scorned to live solely on inherited wealth, and the sense of responsibility that worked in order to provide work for others, in a community that might lose its population and its identity if its people had to leave their birthplace behind in order to seek a living elsewhere. Julian had every excuse not to work, and Dan could easily earn a living if he had to by sketching alone, his draughtsmanship had in it a spark of genius that lifted his work—and his second love, after the *Kittiwake*—above the level of a mere hobby.

'Oh, do leave me alone!' She spoke aloud in angry despair. No matter how hard she tried, Dan Penderick was never far from her thoughts. She could not dismiss him from her mind as she wanted to. She had entered his home, and against her will he had entered her heart.

'Oh, how lovely!' Suddenly, at her feet, the field of daffodils spread a yellow nodding carpet that immediately lightened her mood. 'I wonder if I could take some back with me.' Dan had said the flower farm was deserted. That meant nobody owned the daffodils, so it would be all right for her to pick them. Further along the cliff, the desolate ruin of a cottage confirmed Dan's statement, and allayed her conscience.

'I'll take some back for Hannah.' They would make a change from the pallid petals and cloying perfume of the narcissus that Tessa had brought with her that morning, and which seemed to pervade the whole entrance hall with their sickly smell that Jo decided she no longer liked.

'These will be more cheerful.' The gay yellow of the tiny cliff field entranced her, and she cast about for the path that must lead down to it.

'It doesn't look as if it's been walked on for years.' Jo glanced at it dubiously when she found the smooth-looking track that dipped steeply into the field below. It would be awkward to negotiate. But probably Tessa had had to climb down a path just as steep to pick her narcissus. What Tessa could do, so could she. The thought spurred Jo on, and with a quick shrug she sat on her heels and shuffled the first few feet downwards, holding on tightly to clumps of greenery growing on either side of her. 'It's not too bad,' she decided. 'Oh, my goodness!' A clump of grass that had looked firmly rooted gave way under her pull, and gravity did the rest. With a speed that took her breath away she started to slide, and before her clutching fingers could find further purchase to brake her progress, she landed in an undignified heap among the daffodils she had come to see.

'Oh, what a shame, I've broken some!' She was lucky she had not broken her limbs as well, she realised, dusting herself down and gazing in awe at the path by which she descended. 'Oh well, I'll find an easier way back when I've picked a bunch to take home.' She checked her thoughts. Penderick House was not her home, and never would be. Maybe it would be Tessa's. Certainly it would be Tessa's, if the girl had her way. With suddenly lowered spirits Jo bent to pick her blooms, choosing the ones just showing yellow from the bud so that they would last longer. A lark rose from the tiny meadow, trilling its joy in the approach of the warmer days, and Jo stood upright for a moment to ease her back. The water sparkled below her, and in it a tiny speck that was Dan's rowing boat butted its way, following the line of the shore.

'Cooee!' Impulsively Jo waved, her spirits restored by her gay handful of flowers, and after a long minute an arm waved back. A small arm—Chris's. Dan did not wave. He probably thought it was beneath his dignity, Jo thought, vexed with herself for drawing attention to her whereabouts in the first place. Or maybe he did not want to loose his oars. Charitably she gave him the benefit of the doubt.

'If it was Tessa he'd have waved,' she told herself forlornly, and watched the rowboat turn about. It headed for the beach, at an abrupt right angle to its previous steady course.

'He's suddenly remembered another lobster pot,' she thought, maliciously glad that Dan was human enough to forget where he had sown it in the first place. Maybe they would have the results of his catch at lunch tomorrow. It would be nice with salad.

The thought of mealtime made Jo look at her watch. She would just be in time for lunch if she started back now. She could stroll along the cliff tops and enjoy the view in peace. She eyed the way she had come down with disfavour. It was out of the question for her to return by the same path, the last three or four feet into the field were a sheer drop, fine for descending by, but impossible to backtrack without a boost, and there were no footholds in the smooth sides of the cliff. A sudden prick of fear touched her, and she thrust it aside impatiently. There was bound to be another way up to the top of the cliff from the field. She derided herself for her momentary panic, and strolled slowly as far as the end corner.

'The path must be on the other side.' With hastening steps she walked the other way, and realised with growing dismay that she had descended by the only possible path into the field, which lay on a ledge jutting out from the cliff, over a hundred sheer feet from the shore below.

Dan had not said why the flower farm was deserted. Was this the reason? Perhaps there had been a cliff fall that made access to the flower field impossible, or dangerous.

Realisation of her predicament wrung a small moan of fear from Jo's lips. She was trapped. And it was her own fault.

CHAPTER SEVEN

'DAN!'

Her frightened cry startled a seagull, and it rose squawking from its perch on some unseen ledge below.

'Dan!'

She raced to the edge of the field overlooking the beach and scanned the water anxiously, but Dan and his boat had disappeared.

'I daren't go near the edge. It might give way.' A shiver shook her. If the daffodil field suffered the same fate as her cottage garden, she would not stand a chance.

Her fingers flew to her lips. Was that a rumble? It grew louder, and the aeroplane responsible for the noise droned by overhead, oblivious of her plight. Jo sank to her knees, cold and trembling.

'Dan! Oh, Dan!'

From far off she seemed to hear his voice call her name. The mind under stress did strange things, she reflected, with a detached kind of interest. She needed Dan now as never before, and like a mirage his voice called out to her.

'Jo! For goodness' sake, woman, stop picking those confounded flowers and come away from the edge of the cliff. Have you got no sense?'

It *was* Dan's voice. She was not imagining things. And she did not imagine his mood, either. She got to her feet, her daffodils still clutched in her hands, and ran shakily back across the field to the bottom of the path by which she had descended. Dan's face appeared over the edge and looked down on her, the same as he had looked down into the rock pool, only this time he did not smile.

'What on earth possessed you to climb down there?' His face was black with anger. 'You might have been killed.'

'I c-can't get back.' Her voice trailed off into miserable silence. She no longer felt afraid, now that Dan was here. Yes, she did. A small, separate part of her analysed her feelings. She was not afraid of being trapped on the cliff any more, but she was afraid of Dan's anger. And it needed no intuition on her part to see that he was furious with her.

'Take hold of the end of this rope,' he barked the instruction at her, and tossed down the looped end of a stout rope. It landed at her feet with an uncompromising thud.

'Wh—what for?' She knew, really, and shook at the prospect.

'Slip the loop round your waist,' he returned impatiently. 'It won't pull tight. Then take hold of the rope in both hands. If you lean backwards against the loop, you can walk your way up the cliff face with me pulling you, the way climbers do.'

'Can't you come down here, to me?' However angry he was with her, she longed for the reassurance of his presence at her side.

'No, I can't.' He was not disposed to be comforting. 'If I come down to you we'll both be stranded. Be thankful I saw where you were,' he snapped brusquely. 'Now don't argue,' as she raised a fearful face to his, 'just do as you're told. Chris isn't big enough to pull you up, even if I did come down, and there aren't any trees around to tie the rope to, so you'll just have to help yourself. Maybe the experience will teach you a lesson.' He spoke as if he would have liked to spank her, and Jo bridled at his tone.

'Tell me what to do and I'll do it,' she snapped back, anger overcoming her dread of both the climb and Dan.

'Slip the loop over you, like I said.' She complied with an angry wriggle. 'Now hold on to the rope and I'll take your weight. And for goodness' sake, throw those flowers away!' he glared down at her bunch of daffodils, which she still held in her hands. 'You'll need both hands to hold on to the rope.'

'I came down to get them, and I'm bringing them back with me.' Furious herself, now, she ignored his impatient exclamation, and carefully tucked her bunch of flowers inside the belt of her mac. It did not matter that they dripped fresh, sticky sap down the red waterproof. She disliked the garment anyway, and it gave her an angry satisfaction that it should be the mac Melvin had chosen for her that was spoiled by her adventure.

'Are you ready now?' Dan enquired sarcastically.

'Quite, when you are.' She smiled up at him sweetly, suddenly glad she had annoyed him; for some perverse reason that gave her satisfaction, too. It was shortlived. He pulled on the rope, standing well back from the cliff edge himself, and hauled with all his might.

'Don't pull so fast!' she protested. She felt like a spider, dangling helplessly at the end of a web, and she thrust out frantically with her feet to save herself from being bumped against the cliff face. A piece of rock dislodged itself, and she ducked hastily as it hurtled past.

'Did it touch you?' Dan's enquiry was instant, and strained.

'No, it didn't,' Jo shouted back grimly. 'But it's no thanks to you. Take it a bit slower, can't you? I can pick my way more carefully then.' It was easier for her to choose her path as Dan slackened his efforts and she ascended more gradually, and soon her head was above the cliff top, and she scrambled thankfully on to her knees on the welcome turf.

'Sis!'

'Stay where you are!' Dan checked Chris's rush to help her with a curt command, and the boy halted at once, glancing uncertainly from Dan to Jo and back again.

'Dan . . .' She looked at him beseechingly, her courage suddenly evaporating now that the danger was over.

'You've got to come to us, not us to you.' Dan still stood well back, the end of the rope in his hands. 'Come on, away from the edge.' He pulled on the rope again, forcing Jo to stumble towards him, like a naughty puppy on the end of a lead, that had to be trained. Fury choked her, and she tore at the rope round her waist with angry fingers, struggling to free herself.

'You can slip it off now.' Dan loomed over her, black-browed and angry. 'Though for two pins,' he gritted, 'I'd keep you roped until we got home. That way I know you'd be safe.' He let the rope go slack, and without its support the loop dropped round Jo's ankles. She went to step out of it, and stumbled as it caught her shoe. Instinctively she reached out to Dan for support, and winced as his fingers caught her arm in a hard grip.

'Don't fall flat on your face, on top of everything else,' he growled, and she looked up at him, stung to protest by his manner. His forehead was beaded with perspiration, and compunction stung her, blowing away her anger at the realisation that he had hauled her weight up a sheer cliff face, on his own. He was enormously strong, but even his strength must have felt the strain.

'You dropped your daffs when you came over the top.' The buds had fallen from her belt as she regained the turf, and Chris stepped forward to recover them for her.

'Leave them there.' Dan grabbed the boy's windcheater and held him back. 'How many times have you got to be told—both of you—to keep away from the cliff edge?' he said sternly. 'There's been a rock slide here before, that's what destroyed the path. There might be another at any time. Your posy would turn into a wreath if you got caught up in a cliff fall,' he pointed out baldly.

'Dan, I'm sorry.' Jo blurted it out, the enormity of her own careless action coming home with uncomfortable force. 'I'll walk home by the lanes,' she promised meekly.

'You'll do nothing of the sort,' he retorted. 'You're coming back in the boat with me, where I know you can't get into any more trouble,' and his tone brooked no disobedience.

The cloying perfume of narcissus met her the moment she stepped into the house. She wrinkled her nose in disgust, and marched towards the stairs to get rid of her sticky mac. Dan came in behind her, but she kept resolutely on. He had not spoken on the way back, and she could think of nothing to say to him now. She preferred not to think of the return journey. He hustled her unceremoniously into the rowboat, which rocked alarmingly as he pushed it out into deep water and got aboard himself. She sat with Chris beside her, facing Dan and trying not to look nervously over her shoulders at odd scrabbling sounds that emerged from a wicker pot just behind them. Could lobsters bite their way out of wicker pots? Or was that crabs? Maybe he had a crab in there. She tensed and looked straight in front of her, trying not to see Dan's set face as he pulled strongly at the oars, the muscles on his arms standing out with the rhythmic dip and thrust that drove the boat through the choppy water with a steady progress. The squeak of the rowlocks jeered at the black depression that settled on her like a cloud. The aura of it even reached Chris, so that after a while he stopped twisting round to watch the contents of the wicker pot—whatever they were—and sat silent beside her as Dan turned the boat along the more placid waters of the creek, and pulled up beside the landing stage at the foot of the house lawns.

He did not appear at dinner time. Jo knew he went to feed the birds in the pens, she saw him set off with a bucket of raw fish, but he did not ask her to accompany him. She would have liked to see Flippers again—mutinously she thought of the guillemot by name. Common sense told her that Dan was right about not naming the seabirds he rescued, but a rebel spark of resentment demanded she defy him.

He did not mention where he had been when they met at breakfast the next morning. Talk around the table became general, and Hannah joined in and broached the subject of going into St Mendoc.

'I could do with one or two things,' she decided. 'It seems a pity to serve that nice lobster without proper dressing. And I reckon that pound you've got is burning a hole in your pocket, isn't it?' she smiled indulgently at Chris.

'Can we go with you?' The boy lost interest in his toast and marmalade. 'You promised,' he reminded Dan eagerly. It was amazing how a new day blew away the cobwebs from the day before, for a child, Jo thought wistfully. Beyond a polite 'Good morning', Dan had not addressed a remark directly to her, and she envied Chris his cheerful unconcern as he turned guilelessly to the owner of the *Kittiwake*, certain of a kindly reception.

'So I did.' Dan broke off his talk about mechanical matters with Lance to smile at the boy. 'So I did,' he agreed. 'Will nine o'clock be all right for you, Hannah?' Considerate as always of the older woman's wishes, he turned and waited courteously for her agreement before continuing. 'Nine it is, then, outside the front door. Hannah will sit in front.' He bent a firm eye on Chris. 'You can sit in the back with Jo. What about you, Lance? Didn't you want to come in to the boatyard and check how the *Gull* is coming along?'

'Yes, there's a couple of points I want to talk over with the foreman before they go any further.'

The *Gull*, Jo knew, was a brand new trawler being built at the boatyard in St Mendoc. She had looked forward to seeing it, she had never seen a boat being built before, and this addition to the Penderick fleet would provide her with a unique opportunity. She felt glad Lance was coming with them, she could go with him to the boat-yard without the necessity of asking Dan.

'Gosh, I didn't know it was this rough!' Chris staggered laughing against his sister as they emerged on the front of the house and met a blast of wind that had not been so evident at the back.

'I heard it blowing during the night.' Jo knotted her silk scarf more securely under her chin.

'The wind started to rise just before dawn.' Dan joined them on the gravel sweep. 'You wouldn't find the rowboat so much fun today,' he told Chris. 'If you look between the trees there, you can see the spray from the breakers on the end of Penderick Head.' He pointed and Chris and Jo watched as a white sheet of spray broke like a fountain, showing up against the dark trees.

'Is that what I heard booming during the night?' Jo forgot her antagonism and turned to Dan, as interested as Chris.

'That would be it. Did it disturb you?' His tone was casually friendly, following her lead. 'You'll have to get used to it, we can't stop the sound of the sea.'

She would not be at Penderick House long enough to get used to it, Jo thought, but she did not say so out loud. It looked as if Dan was prepared to call a truce, and she was glad enough of the easier atmosphere between them while she was under his roof.

'The wind's making the tide run.' Hannah cast a know-ledgeable eye on the shore as the car climbed away from the house and took the road to St Mendoc.

'That means don't go to the beach today,' Dan said evenly, addressing Jo and Chris over his shoulder from the driving seat, and there was unmistakable command in his voice. 'Do remember what I've said,' he urged, 'and keep away from the shore while the wind's as strong as it is now. When the tide's being driven like this it comes in faster than a man can run, and if you get caught in the undertow there's nothing could save you. Did you hear what I said?' His voice sharpened, demanding their compliance.

'We did, and we won't go near the shore. Either of us,' Jo promised. Dimly she perceived his sense of responsibility to herself and Chris while they were his guests, and the anxiety her foolhardiness had caused him yesterday.

'Better still, stay with Hannah,' Dan insisted. 'I know you'll both be all right, then.'

'I'm not a child!' She bridled at his suggestion that she needed an escort.

'You behaved like one yesterday,' he shot back at her grimly, and she flushed furiously. Did he have to remind her, and in front of Hannah and Lance, too?

'That field's a menace,' Hannah put in unexpectedly. 'It attracts all sorts of people when it's in bloom. Oh, the locals know enough to stay away and let the daffs be,' she acknowledged, 'but you're not the first stranger to be caught in that manner,' she comforted Jo. 'Up to now all that it's given the poor souls has been a bad fright, but these rock falls that the frost and the rain started over the last few months, they've made it impossible for anyone to get back once they've jumped down. It was difficult before, but it could be done. Melanie's been down there, and not all the talking to by her father made any difference. It'll take a life one day, that field will, and then perhaps someone will do something,' she finished grimly.

'I'll speak to the Council about it,' Dan promised, his tone quieter now. 'With a bit more sunshine like yesterday it'll bring the visitors down early, and there were still a lot of flowers in the field in tight bud. If the place is securely fenced off as a temporary measure, it'll keep people away until something permanent can be done.'

'It seems a pity to destroy the flowers.' Jo mourned their possible loss. From the sea they had been like a light on the dark cliffs.

'They're not worth someone's life,' Dan retorted sharply. 'It was only by pure coincidence I knew where to look for you yesterday. If you hadn't waved to us no one would have had a clue where to look for you.'

'Well, you'll know where we are today,' Hannah cut across the suddenly tight atmosphere. 'In the bookshop—at the grocers——'

'And at the hotel for a coffee afterwards,' said Lance. 'Don't forget,' he warned them, 'as near to eleven as you can make it. The cream cakes they serve with their coffee are lovely.' Craftily he ensured that Chris would not forget, and would see to it that the women were not allowed to, either. 'Where are you going first, Dan?' he asked his brother.

'To get that engine bit. I can go to the Council afterwards,' Dan answered. 'I'm tired of having to nurse the *Kittiwake* over every patch of rough water. I tried to turn a piece myself, but I couldn't get it to work smoothly, and I didn't want to risk it.'

Was that why he had been up before dawn and knew when it first started to blow? Jo wondered. Or perhaps where he had been the previous evening? She felt suddenly a lot more cheerful. She had taken it for granted he had been with Tessa.

'I'll go and see the foreman at the boatyard.' Lance snapped the lock on the car as they disembarked in St Mendoc's main street. 'What about you, Jo?'

'Chris and I will—why, whatever's that?' Jo came to an abrupt halt and raised startled eyes to the clock tower that loomed above them, incongruous in the middle of the narrow main street.

'We shan't be going anywhere for a bit,' Dan told his brother grimly. 'Have the car keys, Hannah,' he handed them over. 'It'll save you from having to carry your shopping with you. We'll come back as soon as we can, and you can wait for us at the hotel. Treat yourself to a lunch if we're over late.' He smiled at her, and briefly placed a reassuring hand on her shoulder. 'Come on, Lance,' he called, and together the two men ran. Other figures—blue-jerseyed, rubber-booted figures—ran too, all from different directions, from places that Jo had not noticed contained people. Their silent, purposeful running struck a strange terror in Jo's heart, heightened by the sudden banshee wailing coming from the clock tower.

'That's the siren,' Hannah said quietly, and something in her tone made the sense of dread worse. 'It sounds a warning to the crew of the lifeboat that they're needed,' she explained.

'The lifeboat?' Chris's face lit up with excitement. 'Ooh, can we see it go out?'

'Yes, if you're quick. They don't waste time once the warning's gone. You can see it well enough from the end of the street.' She took hold of the boy's hand, evidently taking Dan's caution seriously in case the child should run down to the shore, forgetting in the excitement of the moment the promise the man extracted from them. 'Hold my hand, and help me along,' she suggested tactfully. 'My legs aren't as spry as they used to be.' Just the same she more than kept up with Chris, and Jo felt herself panting as she hurried along beside the two.

'I wish that awful noise would stop.' The insistent summons of the siren wailed on and on, and Jo put frenzied palms to her ears to try and blot it out. Added to the crash of the waves against the sea wall ahead of them, that had been muted by the windows of the car, the violence of the noise hurled a symphony of desperation over the tiny fishing community that brought the people out into the street, hurrying in the same direction as themselves, to stand on the street corner and watch the lifeboat launched. A poster flapped, partly torn off the billboard by the wind, and Jo looked at it indifferently. At any other time it would have caught her eager interest. It advertised a cottage for sale in St Mendoc. But not now.

She cast a glance at the faces around her—all women— and found in them the same as she saw in Hannah's face, a tense waiting, watchful, alert, and yet curiously resigned. No one spoke. Jo had experienced something similar once before, years ago, when she and her father had been in a mining village at the end of a lecture tour, and been the unhappy witnesses of a pit disaster. The same stoicism was there; the same frozen acceptance of what was, that allowed of neither hope nor despair, but watched quietly until the outcome should become known.

'They're away!'

Chris's call broke the silence, and a small murmur rose from the women. One or two men, all elderly, joined the fringes of the little knot of people. One had on a white apron, and carried a knife and steel in his hand, marking him as the local butcher. He must have been in the act of sharpening his tool when the warning sounded.

Slowly at first, then with gathering speed, the lifeboat ran down the slips, the men in it anonymous in their dark oilskins. Jo closed her eyes. It looked too small to survive in the wild water that broke in huge white combers on the beach. For a second it disappeared, and she felt as if her heart had stopped.

'Dan, oh, Dan!' Her cry came from her heart, but it did not pass her lips. All the resentment; all the antagonism fled as if they had never been. The *Kittiwake* was big beside the lifeboat, and even Dan's strength was not proof against the power of the water.

'For those in peril on the sea . . .'

The lines of the familiar hymn came to her with a force of meaning they had never held before, and standing there on the street corner, buffeted by the wind, and half deafened by the noise from the waves, she watched the tiny pencil line that was the lifeboat lift and ride the waves, and slowly work its way against them out to sea. Her hand sought Hannah's, inpulsively reaching out for comfort, and she prayed.

She was not alone among that silent crowd to do the same, she knew. Other women—perhaps the slight, raven-haired girl, heavy with child, who stood next to her, yet silently apart—had her man on the lifeboat as well. Only Dan did not belong to Jo. She had not the right to call him her own, to watch for his return, and fly to his arms with heady relief that he was home.

'How do they stand it?' she whispered, her own control cracking under the unnatural silence, and the strain.

'It's their life.' Hannah's keen ears caught her words. 'It was mine too, once.'

Hannah's husband had been a fisherman, a skipper on one of the Penderick trawlers. Julian told Jo the story one evening, the very lack of emphasis in his gentle voice adding horror to the dreadful reality of what he said.

'They foundered off the Claw Rocks. The boat holed, and sank with all hands. That's what made my father put the light on the end of Penderick Head, and we've maintained it ever since.'

'Come on, there'll be nothing to see now until the boat comes back.' Hannah kept a firm hold of Chris as the lifeboat rounded the end of the headland and dropped out of sight. 'We might as well go and get our shopping done,' she insisted, 'and then we'll be in time to meet them for coffee at the hotel before we go home.' For a brief moment her glance locked with that of the dark-haired girl beside Jo.

The older eyes were full of compassion, the young ones full of sudden tears. Jo longed to help her, but it was not her world. To this girl she was a mere bystander, and she dared not let her own anguish show, not even to Hannah.

'Let's go and get your book, and then we can help Hannah carry the groceries back to the car.' Activity helped. It stopped her from thinking, stopped her from hearing Julian's voice repeat the words of Hannah's story. 'The boat holed, and sank with all hands...'

Choosing his bird book temporarily diverted Chris's attention, and he tucked it under his coat unrebuked when he found it raining as they came outside.

'We'll drop the groceries in the car and go and have our coffee. There's an observation lounge at the hotel that looks right out over the bay, it gives you a much better view than from the street,' Hannah successfully fended off any reluctance on Chris's part. 'Do you know what the boat's gone out to?' she asked the waiter who brought their refreshments.

'They say it's a cabin cruiser in trouble off the Claw,' the man replied. 'Why not take your cake and lemonade into the observation lounge, sonny?' he suggested. 'You might be able to follow the course of the lifeboat from there.'

'It's ghoulish,' Jo protested, but the man, who looked as if he might have a family of his own, shook his head with a smile.

'At that age they only see the drama and excitement. I expect he's planning to be a lifeboatman when he grows up,' he said indulgently. 'Next week he'll probably want to be an astronaut.' There was a touch of envy in his voice.

'Drink your coffee, Miss Jo.' Without asking, Hannah spooned sugar into Jo's cup as well as her own. 'Worritin' won't help them,' she said sensibly. 'It didn't help my man, and it won't help yours.'

'How did you know?' Jo stared at her numbly.

'Bless you, it's as plain as a pikestaff to them as is fond of you, child,' Hannah returned softly. 'And I'm that,' she admitted, 'though I've not known you for long. You're the daughter I never had.' Her faded eyes gazed back at the lost years. 'The boys have been like sons to me, I was lucky to have them, but I always wanted a girl...'

'Oh, Hannah, what can I do?' Now Hannah knew her secret, there was no point in pretending.

'There's nothing you can do, except wait,' her companion shook her head sadly. 'The Penderick men do their own choosing. Mr Dan will make up his mind in his own good time.' Unerringly she knew it was Dan, and not Julian or Lance.

'I can't stop loving him.' Tears choked Jo's voice. 'And I don't even know if it would work out. I don't know if I could stand the strain. Today...'

'That's something only you can decide,' Hannah said sagely.

'Is it always like this?'

'It's always like this with men of the sea.' The fisherman's widow offered no false comfort. 'The men put out to sea and the women wait on the shore. It's always been like that, and it always will.'

'I didn't know Dan and Lance were lifeboatmen.'

'All the younger men hereabouts serve the boat. Amos did, and Roddy will when it comes his turn.'

Jo stared at her uncomprehending.

'And the women let them go?'

'That way, the women serve too.'

'Should I have the strength?' Jo whispered. She had asked herself that once before.

'If you haven't, you're best away from it,' Hannah told her quietly. 'There's some things have to be accepted to be borne. If you can't accept his way of life, leave him alone, or it'll end in misery for both of you. I've seen it happen before, and I wouldn't want it to happen to you. Or to Mr Dan.'

'I want to be a lifeboatman,' Chris announced, rejoining them. 'Roddy'n me'll take over when Dan and Lance are too old,' he decided seriously.

'Dan needn't go,' Jo began tentatively. 'You said he needn't fish for a living.'

'The sea's his life, not his living,' Hannah corrected her. 'Part him from his boats, and it'd be like taking his sight away. The lifeboat for him is just a natural extension of the *Kittiwake*. The one helps to keep the other, in fact.'

'How do you mean?' Jo wasn't really interested, but talking helped to pass the endless minutes. It was the *Kittiwake*'s master who interested her, not the boat, but it seemed as if the one was inseparable from the other.

'Any profit the *Kittiwake* makes over and above her own running costs goes to the lifeboat station,' Hannah told her. 'The coast's wild hereabouts, we get a lot of storms, and it means heavy running costs for the lifeboat station. They've got the very latest boat,' she added proudly. 'They commissioned it last year, that's why the *Gull* had to wait another year to be built.'

No wonder the three brothers had been so interested in the amount their catch would fetch. Enlightenment dawned on Jo. She had not been able to understand why Dan and Lance chose such hard dangerous work when it was not strictly necessary.

'They're brave.' Hero-worship shone in Chris's eyes.

'Aye, they're brave,' Hannah acknowledged. 'They've both got a Royal National Lifeboat Institution's award for gallantry, and those awards aren't won for nothing.'

'They never said . . .'

'They wouldn't. And when they come back, you're not to tell them I told you,' she cautioned the boy. 'They're on their way now—look.' She turned Chris's attention out of the wide glass-panelled lounge.

'There's two boats.' Chris glued his nose to the pane. 'Oh, can't we go down and see them in? Please?' he begged.

'Take the lad down,' Hannah bade Jo. 'I'll stay on here, they'll want a quick meal and finish their business here before they go back home now, time's getting on.'

'Come on Jo, do!' Chris tugged impatiently at her sleeve.

'There's plenty of time,' Hannah said calmly. 'Don't forget, the boat's not only got to make its own way in, it's towing the other as well. It'll slow them down a lot.'

'Just the same,' Jo stood up, as eager to be away as her brother, 'we'll go and watch them come in.' For the moment she had almost ceased to care whether Dan loved her or not—almost—so long as he stepped safely ashore. Once she'd seen him again, it would matter ...

'Hey, slow down! Hannah said there's no need to rush.'

'Sorry.' Remorsefully Jo checked her speed, but it was with a sigh of relief she reached the street corner where they had stood and watched the boat being launched.

'We're not the first.'

Several more women were there. The young expectant mother was one. And now the women talked among themselves. Not of the job their menfolk had put to sea to do, Jo noticed, nor yet of their own relief at their imminent return. They spoke casually of mundane things. The cost of children's shoes. 'They don't last 'im five minutes, the young rip, and you can't stop 'em playing hopscotch, can you?' One had got a new knitting pattern, and bemoaned its complications.

'It seems quieter.' Was it only her imagination, or was the roar of the waves against the sea wall less than it was? Jo listened, trying to decide.

'The tide's on the turn.' The dark-haired girl volunteered the information, and her eyes smiled in a friendly fashion, no longer remote, locked in her own anguished fear. 'The force has gone out of the water.'

'They'll be in in about twenty minutes,' the middle-aged woman who had grumbled about the price of shoes turned purposefully. 'I'll go and put the dinner on.'

'I've cooked ours,' the young wife admitted.

'You'll soon learn to time it better.' Her companion went off in the direction of home, but the dark-haired girl lingered, standing with Jo and Chris until, with what seemed an impossible effort, the two boats tied up and after a short wait a knot of blue-jerseyed figures emerged from the life-boat station and broke up to go their different ways as they reached the corner of the main street. A young fresh-faced man, his hair as fair as his wife's was dark, came up and took her arm.

'I'm hungry.'

'Your dinner's spoiled.'

'Never mind, love, it'll go down well just the same.'

Their voices faded, and there was Dan and Lance, safe and sound and walking towards her. Lance turned to call something to the young couple, and Dan walked on. Jo could feel his eyes on her across the width of the street. They held hers, as they had done on the *Kittiwake*, but this time she did not want to look away. She gazed back at him as if she could not look enough, reassuring herself over and over again that he was safe.

'Dan . . .' She half stepped towards him, unable to quite check her relief, and his eyes lit up with a smile.

'You shouldn't have waited all this time,' he scolded, but gently, he did not sound cross. 'You must be frozen.' He reached out and cupped his hands over hers. They were warm and strong, and wonderfully alive. Her own tingled with the touch of them. 'I didn't think when we went—

when the siren sounded...' His voice held an odd sort of compunction, and Jo wondered why. He had told her to stay with Hannah. He must have known she would do as he asked, she had given him her word.

'I haven't been here, not all the time. We went to the hotel with Hannah.' She was quick to justify herself. 'But when we saw the boat coming back I—I had to——' she stumbled to a stop, and now her eyes faltered shyly.

'It's all over now,' he told her softly. 'There was nothing to be frightened of, really.' Tessa would probably have known that. She had not, and the strain had been consequently greater. It showed in her tense figure and haunted eyes that sought his again, unable to quite believe their own evidence, that he stood safely before her. He squeezed her hand reassuringly. 'I'll tell you all about it later,' he promised. 'But not now. Later, when we're ...'

'Did you say Hannah was still up at the hotel?' Lance caught his brother up and interrupted whatever it was he had been about to say. 'I'm starving!' he declared, boyishly.

'Hannah stayed at the hotel to order lunch for all of us.' I'm doing it myself, now, Jo thought, half hysterically. Talking about food when—when—her own voice sounded calm and practical in her ears, and yet how could it, when her feelings were in such a turmoil? And what was Dan going to say? Fervently Jo wished Lance had let him finish.

'I won't come up for lunch with you.' Dan loosed her hand, he seemed to let it go reluctantly, and immediately her fingers felt icy cold again, but it was the coldness of desolation, it had nothing to do with the weather. 'I've got to see the Council people about getting that field fenced off, the sooner that's done the better, before there's an accident, and their offices aren't open after mid-afternoon. I daren't leave it. And then there's the engine bit to be collected. I want to check to make sure it's the right one,' he shook his head as Lance offered to go for him.

'All right, we can meet at the car park about four, then,' Lance said casually. 'Come on, young 'un,' he grasped Chris's shoulder, 'you and I'll have to eat Dan's lunch between us.'

'Don't wait for me in case I'm delayed.' Dan looked searchingly at Jo. 'If you get any colder you'll be sneezing by morning,' he prophesied. 'Take the car back, Hannah's got the keys. I'll get a lift home with Julian, we'll be home in time for dinner.' And he left them, striding up the steep, cobbled street, the street that Julian found it difficult to walk up when it was wet.

And that was that. No eager hug of greeting, not even from the dark-haired girl for her young husband. She must have longed to throw her arms about him, as much as Jo longed to embrace Dan. Her own arms ached now with emptiness, but she took her cue from the other girl's behaviour, which brought home to her more forcibly than perhaps anything else could have done the truth of Hannah's words. The young husband had received no joyous greeting, just, 'Your dinner's spoiled,' and he had replied in kind. A casual resumption of their everyday life, as if nothing untoward had happened. Would she ever be able to do the same? Jo wondered. Would she be able to accept Dan's way of life? Hannah had said it must be accepted to be borne or left alone altogether. To share him willingly with the *Kittiwake*, and the element that sustained it? Or leave him behind, and cut him out of her life for ever?

Once again she asked herself the question. Would she have the strength to do either?

CHAPTER EIGHT

'EAT your cabbage. Sailors get scurvy if they don't eat plenty of greens.' Lance took blatant advantage of Chris's new plans for when he was grown up.

'I don't want to be a sailor. I want to be a lifeboatman, same's you.'

'I thought I recognised you as one of the men on the lifeboat. I didn't get the chance to thank you properly for the tow you gave us this morning.' An affected drawl cut across their conversation, and a man and girl paused by their table. Both wore yachting gear, brand new from the look of it, Jo noticed observantly, and both of them looked as if they would have been more at home sunning themselves on the beach of some fashionable Mediterranean resort than in the lounge of St Mendoc's only hotel.

'Caused quite a bit of excitement, what?' drawled the man, leaning languidly against the back of Hannah's chair, and bringing a frown of disapproval to that worthy's face.

'Meet the master and crew of the cabin cruiser we brought in just now.' Lance's voice was dry. 'Another quarter mile and the current would have pulled you straight on to the Claw Rocks.' He looked directly at the man, his manner holding more than a hint of Dan's sternness. 'I don't think you would have found the consequences exciting then,' he added curtly, and the man flushed, and straightened away from Hannah's chair. She settled her hat like an angry hen settling its feathers, and gave a disapproving sniff.

'I say, you can't blame a body for running out of fuel,' the man protested, his condescending manner wilting slightly under the joint disapproval. 'Two double Scotches, waiter.' He snapped his fingers arrogantly, and brought a scowl to the erstwhile pleasant visage of the waiter.

'Do you mean to say you didn't check your fuel before you set out?' Disbelief choked Lance's utterance for a minute, and the girl spoke up defensively.

'Why should we bother? The fellow who sees to the boat said he'd have it ready. He's paid to do that kind of thing.'

'All tanked up, he said,' her escort confirmed.

'Of course, we did set off an hour or two earlier than we said we would, darling,' the girl giggled. 'It was all a bit of a lark, really. Wait till we get home and tell them!' She gave Lance a ravishing smile. 'They'll all be jealous that we've been rescued by such a handsome bunch. But we were so busy looking at that cluster of birds on the water, we didn't really notice we were in any danger, and then the engine passed out. It's a good job you knew how to use the radio, you clever boy,' she simpered to her companion.

'What birds were those?' Lance struggled to be polite.

'Oh, I don't know, they could have been anything. They were all covered in oil, the poor dears.'

'Oil?' Lance sat up, giving her all his attention now. 'Whereabouts did you see them?'

'Oh, about half a mile out from where you took us in tow,' the man told him as the girl shrugged indifferently. He looked relieved at the change of subject.

'Did you pick them up?'

'Good heavens, no!' the girl grimaced her distaste. 'I told you, they were all covered in oil. They'd have made the deck dirty. Daddy'll be cross enough as it is that we've taken his boat in the first place.'

'Your whiskies, sir.' The waiter drew their attention just in time to prevent Lance's feelings from boiling over.

'I detest painted fingernails.' He vented his wrath on the first thing he remembered as they emerged from the hotel, leaving Hannah in the lounge chatting to a crony, with a firm promise to be at the car park by four, while Jo and Chris accompanied him to the boatyard.

'Fancy leaving those birds!' He could not forget the callous behaviour of the pair he had recently helped to rescue, and he strode forward with angry steps.

'Afternoon, Lance,' a voice hailed them from what Jo had taken to be a large warehouse close against the beach. 'Heard you took the boat out, this morning.' A man rounded the door with a saw in his hands, and nodded in a friendly fashion to Jo and Chris.

'A cabin cruiser. They ran out of fuel.' Incredulity still rang in Lance's voice. 'Anyhow, while we were here I thought I'd run over a few things with you about the *Gull*.' Evidently this was the boatyard, and the man chatting to them was the foreman Lance intended to see.

'Ooh look, Jo, you can see its ribs!' Chris peered round the door and his eyes widened at the skeleton of the boat confronting him.

'It's the cladding I've come to see you about, among other things. Go ahead and have a look, Jo,' Lance added, 'you won't be in the way. Now, I'd thought of having ...' The two men slowly walked round the boat, deep in conversation, and Jo gazed about her, fascinated by the birth of a new vessel. Dan's boat. Still only half finished, and landlocked on the boatyard, it looked somehow pathetic. It was hard to believe it would soon ride the sea as proud as the *Kittiwake* and obedient to its master's command. For the first time, Jo sensed something of the pride Dan must feel in his boat. Perhaps he had watched the *Kittiwake* being built, maybe taken her on her maiden voyage, and so forged a link that made the boat peculiarly his own. Would he give the *Kittiwake* to Lance when this one was built, and take over the *Gull* when she was ready? If he did it would grant Lance's dearest wish, to skipper a boat of his own.

Absorbed in what she saw, she followed Chris slowly

round the structure, and stopped abruptly as they came to the big double doors again, and found Amos leaning against the doorpost.

'Have you come to see how she's getting along, Amos? 'Twon't be long before she's commissioned.' The foreman appeared as well and smiled at Jo. 'Lance won't be long, miss, he's making a couple of phone calls to the component suppliers. His word will carry more weight then mine.'

Because he was a Penderick. But if the family held a position of authority, it had been hard won, and the universal respect they received from the community in which they lived was only their due, and it no longer aggravated her.

'He'll be here to give you a lift home any minute,' the man added cheerfully.

'We're living with Dan Penderick.' Chris made it abundantly clear that Lance's home was also theirs, and he did it in a most ill-chosen manner.

'That could be true.' A voice, barbed with malice, turned Jo and the two men around, and Jo groaned. Tessa again. She had a shopping basket in her hand; probably she thought Dan had come down to the boatyard, and came herself in the hope of meeting him.

Well, she'll be disappointed this time, Jo thought grimly. There was no doubt the girl had heard what Chris said, and put the worst possible construction on his innocent words. Her face went white with anger. Even her lips lost their normal healthy colour.

'Well, now . . .' The foreman looked heartily embarrassed, not knowing how to cope with the situation. Amos had greater faith in his own capabilities.

'On your way home, gel.' His face was stern, and he waved his pipe at Tessa in angry dismissal. 'Get off with you. Now!' he ordered.

'Oh, very well, I know when I'm not wanted. And Dan's

not here anyhow.' She flashed Jo a glance of pure malice and flounced off, and the old fisherman stuck his pipe back between his teeth and looked straight at Jo.

'Tek no notice o' that one, wench,' he told her, and this time his growl had a kindly sound to it. 'She's no leddy herself, and don't know when she sees one. Aye!' With this pronouncement he stamped off, whether to see that Tessa had obeyed his order or not he did not say. 'See you later at the Anchor,' his voice called back to the foreman, and Lance grinned as he joined them.

'Did I hear Amos call you wench?' he asked interestedly, and when Jo nodded, 'You *are* honoured,' he assured her. 'He only calls a woman wench if he really likes her.' His eyes laughed, but his voice was quite serious, and strangely Jo knew he meant what he said. 'Heavens, is that the time?' He caught sight of the clock on the workshed wall. 'Come on, we'll have to hurry if we're not to keep Hannah waiting. You can come and have a look at the *Gull* another time.' He took Jo's arm, and calling to Chris hurried her away in the direction of the parked car. 'In the meantime, try practising breaking a bottle of champagne over her bows. In imagination, of course,' he corrected himself with a grin. 'We'll give you the real job on the day,' he promised.

Jo doubted it. That job would go to Tessa, not herself. But she did not say so to Lance. He liked Melanie well enough, but somehow she felt he did not care for Tessa very much; there was a reservation in the younger man's manner when Tessa was around that was not evident in Dan.

'We've just made it,' Chris triumphed, gesturing towards where Hannah walked purposefully towards the car, but still some yards distant. 'There's Melanie with her.' He waved, and the young girl broke into a run.

'I've come to see your bird book,' she panted to a stop. 'Hannah said it cost a whole pound.' Her voice held awe.

'I earned it, crewing on the *Kittiwake*.' Chris tugged it

from under his coat. 'It's all wrapped up now. Come home with us and have a look at it there, we can sit on the rug and see it together.'

'Chris! It's not home to us. You mustn't...' Jo went scarlet with embarrassment and Lance laughed.

'It's home for now,' he said easily, 'that's good enough. And it's been second home to this one since she could toddle,' he tugged a lock of Melanie's dark hair in an older brother fashion. 'Come back with us if you want to, Sprite, I expect Hannah will let you stay to tea. That is, if it will be O.K. with Tessa?' he added dutifully.

'She said I could stop out until supper time.' Melanie squeezed into the car with Chris. Probably Penderick House had been home from home with both the girls, Jo thought. Tessa would be much of an age with the two younger Penderick men, probably they had played together as children. Been invited to the same parties, and so on.

'I can't stop thinking of those birds,' Lance decanted Hannah and the two young people at the front door of Penderick House. Chris and Melanie raced up the front steps, unable to wait to examine their new treasure, and Hannah followed at a more leisurely pace, her motherly voice calling after them to, 'Mind and wipe your feet now, both of you!'

'Neither can I,' Jo admitted. 'Will the boats see them when they go out tonight, do you think?' It was a possibility, but not very probable after dark.

'Not a hope,' Lance confirmed her doubts. 'And it'll be hours before Dan gets back. It's only just gone four now, and dinner isn't until eight, that means over three hours away.'

'The water seems calm enough now.' Miraculously it was. The tide had turned, the wind dropped to a brisk breeze, and although there was a heavy swell running, the sea had the aspect of a millpond in comparison to its angry behaviour of the morning.

'I'm going out to fetch those birds in.' Lance made up his mind.

'But how can you? Dan's not here.'

'I don't need Dan breathing down my neck every time I put to sea.' The youngest Penderick bridled. 'I'm as capable as he is of taking the *Kittiwake* out.'

'The *Kittiwake*?' Jo looked at him aghast. 'Lance, you can't! You mustn't. The *Kittiwake*'s Dan's boat. He'll be furious.'

'He should let me skipper one of my own.' His young jaw set stubbornly. 'He knows I'm capable, he just won't admit it. Don't worry, there's no danger,' he assured her as she still looked worried. 'It won't put the boat at risk. The storm's blown itself out, and there's no excuse to leave those birds out there to die.' Impulsively he grasped her arm. 'Come with me and crew for me, Jo,' he begged her. 'There'll be nothing for you to do except help me fish them out of the water,' as she demurred. 'I need someone to hold the other end of the net. Tomorrow it might be too late to save them, even if we could find them by then. Dan would go in a minute, if he was here,' he coaxed.

'Very well, I'll come.' She slid back hastily into the car, before she had time to change her mind. 'Lucky I went out in slacks, it'll save changing.' She kept pace with Lance as he parked the car and ran along the harbour wall.

'There's the *Sea Swallow*, tied up alongside the *Kittiwake*,' she pointed to the boats moored by the harbour steps. If they took the *Sea Swallow*, maybe Dan would not be angry. Even now she regretted her impulsive agreement to accompany Lance.

'Take Amos's boat?' Lance looked at her in genuine amazement. 'I wouldn't dare,' he confessed. 'Amos would never forgive me if I took a woman aboard his boat.'

And Dan won't forgive you—or me—in a hurry, for taking the *Kittiwake*, Jo realised unhappily, but it was too late now. She grasped Lance's hand, her feet hurrying down the wet stone steps, and then she was on the deck of Dan's boat, and Lance untied it and joined her with a quick, practised leap that judged the widening gap between the harbour wall and the boat rails to a nicety.

'Come on into the wheelhouse, it's warmer there.' He drew her into the tiny enclosure, and with hands as sure as those of his brother he guided the trawler out between the arms of the harbour, and turned to follow the coastline.

'The birds can't be all that far out,' he murmured. 'I reckon they'll be about half a mile off the Claw, still.'

'I thought you said there was a current that pulled towards the rocks?' Jo remembered his remark to the man at the hotel.

'So there is, but from what that idiot from the cabin cruiser told us, I reckon the birds must have been beyond the pull of it, and the ebb tide will probably drift them further out still.'

'Do you think Dan will mind?' she began tentatively, her misgivings returning with full force now she had nothing to occupy her.

'I don't care whether he minds or not,' Lance retorted carelessly. 'I'm not going to let those birds die for the sake of trying to get them back. Keep a look out for'ard,' he instructed her, 'we shall soon be in the area where they were seen, and they could have drifted in any direction.'

Dutifully, Jo looked, but all she could see was the heaving water, and in it a reflection of Dan's face, angry as it had been when he pulled her back from the daffodil field, and with a queer, sick feeling inside her she wished heartily Lance had not talked her into coming with him. Sick? Oh no, she mustn't be seasick as well. That would be the last straw. And incur Dan's wrath for yet another reason. Tension turned her stomach into a tight ball, and she regretted the ice cream and trifle she had rashly indulged in at lunch time. It had seemed like a tiny celebration then, because Dan was safely back.

'There they are.' Lance's more accustomed sight picked out a dark patch on the water ahead. 'I'll get as near as I can to them.' He throttled the engine down. It gave an odd sort of cough and settled into a muffled thump that just gave the boat way against the swell. Lance ran out on to the deck and Jo followed him, Dan's possible disapproval temporarily forgotten. Lance had judged their position well; the birds were coming up alongside, but so slowly they had ample time to unravel the net between them.

'Lower it when I say.' It was suitably weighted, and hung down just above the water.

'They look in a bad way.' Jo peered over the side.

'Aye.' His reply was brief, as grim as Dan's had been on a similar, earlier mission.

'Now!' Lance flung his end of the net outwards and down, all that Jo had to do was hold on to her side of it, which she did with all her might, finding it unexpectedly heavy as it hit the water and sank.

'We've got them!'

'All of them?'

'Yes, lift up. Gently,' he bade her. It was heavier still now, but with a mighty effort she managed it.

'Best leave this bit to me. Go and have a look over the other rail for a minute.' Considerately Lance took on the grisly task of sorting out their catch, and for once Jo was glad to do as she was told. One glance at the net confirmed the queasy feeling inside her, and she dared not let it get the upper hand. After a few minutes, from behind her she heard a series of faint splashes, then Lance's voice again.

'Four of them were dead. These others might survive, with luck.' He carried the rest of the birds back to the wheelhouse and laid them side by side in the basket under the locker. 'We'll get back home and wash them clean.' He reached for the controls and throttled the engine into life again. For a couple of seconds it responded, and then suddenly it gave another cough, and with what Jo suspected was a death rattle, it died into ominous silence.

'Come on, old girl . . .' Lance spoke impatiently and tried again. 'Oh——!' He gave a muttered expletive. 'Just as I wanted to be extra quick.' He did not say whether he wanted to be quick for the sake of the birds, or to be back in harbour before Dan came home. Jo's own feelings included a good measure of the latter.

'Can you get it going again?' Her voice was tight.

'Of course I can,' he replied confidently. 'It's just that bit playing up again, I've adjusted it before.' He dropped down into the hold, and Jo's anxious ears caught various metallic sounds that indicated a spanner being wielded.

'It's no good.' He reappeared several minutes later, and his confident air was replaced by a worried frown. 'You know that bit Dan said he'd tried to turn for himself, and it didn't quite fit?'

Jo nodded dumbly, dreading what was to come.

'Well, he left it on the engine in place of the faulty part. He must have been carrying the old piece with him this morning, to make sure the suppliers had got the exact part.'

'Does that mean . . .?'

'We're stuck,' he found the words for her, and his glance flicked shorewards. Towards the black outline of the Claw Rocks? Jo's throat went dry.

'The current?' she whispered, fearfully, remembering what he had said to the cabin cruiser man that morning.

'We're too far out for the current to touch us, thank goodness,' he replied, but his worried look did not diminish, and Jo wondered fearfully whether he was as confident as he sounded. She searched his face, but found no reassurance there. Lance looked desperately concerned at their plight.

'What shall we do?' Her eyes were enormous, pleading with him to find a solution. What on earth would Dan say when he realised his boat was not only taken, but broken down and stranded? She dreaded to think, and resolutely closed her mind to the many possibilities that presented themselves.

'The lifeboat?' she suggested tentatively. He would be angrier still if they had to turn that out again, twice on the same day, and each time through someone else's carelessness.

'No, not the boat.' Jo noticed they all called it 'the boat', as if there was only one boat in St Mendoc. It was that important, to them.

'We've got ship-to-shore radio, I'll use that. Dan said he was going to the canning factory to join up with Julian, we've got a radio link direct with his office.' He consulted his watch. 'With a bit of luck they'll both be there now.'

'Dan?' She'd prefer the lifeboat, Jo thought worriedly, and then changed her mind. Dan would have to come out on that too, so the one was as bad as the other.

'He'll bring the *Sea Swallow* out, and give us a tow in, I expect.' Lance tried to be comforting.

'That'll confirm all Amos's fears about women on boats,' Jo said miserably. 'And just as he seemed to be getting to like me, too.' She had not forgotten the old fisherman's unexpected championship when Tessa was being spiteful.

'Don't worry about Amos,' Lance echoed Dan's words, but with a different meaning. 'He likes you well enough. He thinks you're a "leddy", he's said so,' he grinned briefly. 'And you needn't worry about those, either,' he nodded towards the Claw Rocks. 'We're too far out, and on the wrong side of them, for the current to take us.'

'I wasn't thinking of the Claw.' Strangely enough, she had not been. She looked at them indifferently. They looked almost friendly she thought ruefully, in comparison with what she was expecting from Dan when they met. With no little trepidation she watched Lance operate the radio. After a lot of crackling a voice answered. Lance gave a curt résumé of their plight, and then Dan's voice came on the air, disembodied, slightly distorted by the atmospherics, but unmistakably Dan. And just as unmistakably, very angry.

'I'll come and fetch you in,' he snapped, and the radio went dead. Lance pulled a face.

'Big brother didn't sound too pleased.'

'He doesn't look it,' thought Jo, peering out of the wheelhouse window half an hour later, and watching from a safe distance as the *Sea Swallow* drew alongside, and a hail from its deck drew Lance outside. She could not hear what the two men said to one another, but a rope was exchanged between the trawlers and Lance made it fast. With a signal of his hand he rejoined Jo in the wheelhouse.

'There'll be a bit of a jerk when it tightens, but it's nothing to worry about,' he told her.

That was the least of Jo's worries, but she did not tell him so. Her throat felt dry, her head felt hot, and she wished her stomach belonged to someone else. She dreaded staying in the wheelhouse, and she dreaded going ashore.

'At least one of us is feeling chirpy,' Lance commented more cheerfully, as a rustling from the basket on the floor attracted their attention to one of its occupants, that had struggled upright and was now taking interested stock of its new surroundings. 'Cheer up, Jo,' he continued bracingly. 'Dan can't eat us,' he assured her. 'He might even be pleased, when he sees the birds.'

Dan looked quite capable of swallowing both of them, she thought shakily. She emerged reluctantly on to the deck as the two boats closed on their moorings, and the men tied up. She tried to pick up the basket of birds, but as she bent down her head began to swim and she hurriedly straightened up again.

'I'll take those.' Lance evidently thought she found the basket too heavy and she did not disabuse him. Dan was coming aboard, and she wanted her senses clear for the difficult minutes that she felt sure were bound to follow. He did not wait for them to disembark. With a swift twist of the rope he made the *Sea Swallow* fast and leaped with a lithe grace from one boat to the other as surefooted as a cat. With detached interest Jo noticed he wore soft pumps, which accounted for the silence of his tread as he approached them. Somehow it made his approach almost menacing, heightened by the grim silence of his demeanour. It was like the calm before the fury of a storm, Jo thought, and caught her breath.

'Well?' Dan stopped in front of Lance with a curt monosyllable.

'We went out after these,' Lance replied evenly. He tipped the basket slightly so that Dan could see the birds. 'That fellow in the cabin cruiser told us where he'd seen them. I couldn't let them stay out there and die,' he said simply.

'You could have contacted me before you purloined the *Kittiwake*,' Dan grated harshly.

'It would have taken too long to locate you. It seemed more important to go straight out. I didn't think beyond that,' Lance admitted.

'Do you ever think?' Dan snapped back, the heat of his anger beginning to show. 'You knew very well the engine was faulty.'

'I've adjusted it before,' Lance protested, and Dan interrupted him with angry impatience.

'I told you it was good enough in calm water, when it was nursed along. Not in a sea like this. Look at the swell that's running! I'd have thought even you would have had the sense not to risk a boat with a faulty engine on that kind of water,' he snapped contemptuously, and Lance flushed, angry now in his turn.

'How was I to know you'd leave a dud bit on the engine?' he demanded hotly. 'I didn't know you'd taken the original component off as a sample, and of course you didn't think to tell me,' he added sarcastically.

'I don't expect to have to explain my actions on my own boat!' Dan shouted back at him. The two brothers faced one another, each furiously angry, and somewhere beneath the frightened hammering of her heart Jo plucked up enough courage to interrupt them.

'Lance only wanted to save the birds,' she began, and stepped back hastily as Dan turned and glared at her.

'If you hadn't agreed to crew for him he wouldn't have gone out in the first place,' he barked, and she went white at the fury in his face. The sheer injustice of being blamed for something she didn't want to do to start with bolstered her quailing spirit, and she flashed back.

'If you had the sense to warn Lance about the useless part you'd left on the engine, or better still left it off altogether so that the beastly thing wouldn't start anyhow, none of this would have happened,' she raised her voice and shouted right back at him, and surprised herself as much as Dan in the process. In the quiet, academic world that had been her environment until now, she had never felt the need to raise her voice to anybody. It was a new experience to her, and a rather shocking one, she found. But it was exhilarating, too. She had managed to surprise Dan into silence, and Lance, she discovered, was looking at her with a dawning respect in his face. And also a dawning grin. Now was not the time to laugh, and she eradicated it.

'If you two are going to stand there arguing over the rights and wrongs of taking your precious boat out,' she flung at them both, 'the reason for the journey will be wasted anyhow. Something will have to be done about those birds quickly, or they'll die, and I don't relish feeling seasick for nothing.' A stronger than usual qualm from inside her warned her that if she remained on the deck much longer—even here, in the harbour, the water was undeniably heaving up and down in the most uncomfortable manner, and her inner self was doing the same thing—she might lose the advantage of her temporary strength, and give Dan the whip hand again. 'You can stay here all day if you want to,' she said with asperity, 'but I'm going home.' She didn't correct herself, as she had corrected Chris. Anywhere where she could lie down and remain still would be home to her now, she thought wretchedly. She turned her back on Dan, lest he should see her lips suddenly tremble, and took a shaky step towards the rail, that seemed unaccountably a very long way away. Even the flight of stone steps had taken to floating about . . .

'Allow me.' He didn't wait for her to allow him or otherwise. With a quick scoop he picked her up in his arms just as her knees felt about to give way. She closed her eyes as the abrupt change in position from shaky vertical to horizontal threatened disaster, and turned her face into the rough darkness of his jersey, blotting out the light, and the *Kittiwake*, and the unstable, treacherous water, feeling only an immense relief at being able to lie still. Soft steps crossed the deck, she could hear them now she was so close, and she felt herself lifted higher—across the rail of the boat—then up the flight of stone steps. She started to count them, but lost interest before they got to the top. She opened her eyes, then. The breeze from the sea hit them with full force on the top of the harbour wall, and acted as an astringent against her waxen cheeks.

'Put me down, I'm all right now. It was only the steps, they wouldn't stand still.' Did she detect a faint upward curve to Dan's lips as he looked down on her, lying close against his shoulder, but for once he did not argue.

'Try your feet, but hold on to me until you're sure you can manage on your own.' Gently he put her down, and Jo clung to him with both hands. She would have dearly loved to hold her head high and walk away, but physical weakness betrayed her, and a pair of trembling knees cried out for help to support her.

'I think I can manage.' She couldn't. She would never really be able to manage without Dan, now, but it was her heart that was at fault there, not her knees. They seemed immeasurably stronger, and the stability of the harbour wall helped her own. She loosed first one hand, then another experimentally, and found the swimmy feeling did not come back.

'Thank you for the lift.' Her chin rose and she looked at Dan squarely, gathering together the tattered remains of her dignity.

'My pleasure.' He sketched a bow, mocking her, and temper sparked for a moment in her eyes. He spoke as if it was a pleasure, as if he enjoyed the fact that she had been forced to rely on him to support her. Anger completed the restoring effect of the wind, and Jo turned, sure now on her feet, and spoke to Lance curtly.

'Let's go back and look after the birds.' She ignored Dan. She did not care whether he came back with them or not, she hoped he would not. It would give her all the longer to regain her poise. Perhaps he would stay with the *Kittiwake* and put in the new bit he needed for the engine.

'The sooner the better, I think.' The younger man's face was full of concern as he gazed into the basket, his anger forgotten with the urgency of a new task ahead.

'I'll follow you along, I came down in Julian's car.' Neither Lance nor Jo bothered to answer him, Jo did not even look round to see if he was following them, although she twisted round in the passenger seat she kept her eyes on the bedraggled birds and resolutely refused to look out of the back window of the car. A familiar van was parked outside Penderick House when they drew up, and she made a face.

'Tessa's here.'

'Do you want to go in and say hello?' Lance asked. 'I'm not going to bother, I want to give these a wash first,' he indicated the basket.

'I'll come and help you,' Jo said firmly. 'Tessa and I don't seem to have—er—much in common.' She tried to be as polite as possible. They did have one thing in common—Dan—but it was hardly conducive to a good relationship between them.

'I'd noticed your friendship wasn't exactly flourishing,' Lance grinned. 'Melanie's all right, though,' he added, 'she's a nice enough youngster.' Melanie was more Lance's generation than Tessa, who was nearer to Dan's age. And wanted to be a lot nearer to Dan, Jo thought caustically. Well, she could have him! She hurried after Lance, intent on helping him. This time she knew what to expect, and was of more use to Lance than she had been to his brother.

'Flippers is coming along fine.' Defiantly she used her pet name for the guillemot Dan had rescued.

'I think these will if I can get them clean without exhausting them beyond hope.' Lance worked industriously, soaping and cleaning while Jo wielded the shower. 'Let's see if they'll take some food.' He tried the same tactics as his brother, with the same results, except for one bird, 'He's a puffin,' that was too weak to eat. 'I'll try giving him some brandy.' Lance went to lay him down, reluctantly.

'I'll go.' Jo was on her feet immediately. 'Tell me where it is.'

'Hannah keeps it, ask her.' Lance gazed up at her gratefully. 'If we can get him through the night he should pull round all right.' He gazed compassionately at the limp creature in his palms, a travesty of the staid, upright little birds that to Jo always looked as if they only needed a bowler hat and a briefcase to make them the perfect city business types.

'Take him this.' Hannah reached for what was evidently an emergency kit kept specially for the purpose. 'There's a drop of milk—oh, and don't forget the spoon,' she directed. 'A dropper's no good with the sort of bird he's got, one clap of its bill and there'd be glass everywhere.' She handed over a metal spoon and Jo fled for the door, fearful that any second's delay might have an adverse effect.

'Feeling better now?' Dan's voice spun her round as she reached out for the knob. He came out of the drawing room, with Tessa in front of him, and they were both laughing. At her? Jo's face flamed. No doubt her malaise would make a very funny story, she thought furiously. Just the same, it was unforgivable of Dan to tell it for Tessa's entertainment.

'Quite,' she snapped, and deliberately turned her back on both of them, but if her simple manoeuvre shut them from her sight, it did not put her out of earshot, she discovered.

'I can't imagine why Lance took her,' Tessa's voice was deliberately provocative. 'I told her before, she'd be seasick. Trippers always are.' And she laughed again.

CHAPTER NINE

'MELANIE'S had to go home with Tessa.' Chris looked up from the hearthrug as Jo appeared dressed for dinner.

'She said she could only stay out until supper time,' Jo reminded him. So that was Tessa's excuse for coming to Penderick House. She had never known her to come and collect Melanie before, usually the young girl had the long walk back to the flower farm on her own. Evidently Tessa had missed Dan in St Mendoc; Amos must have had his way and seen that she went home when he told her to. And just as obviously Tessa was determined not to be baulked of her intention to see Dan and be with him, if only for a short time, that day. She half smiled as she imagined the other girl's reaction when she found Dan had come out to rescue Lance and herself. She would not be too pleased about that, she thought with malicious satisfaction that was totally unlike her under normal circumstances.

'She liked my book.'

'Mmm?' Jo was only half listening. 'Who?'

'Melanie, of course,' the boy cried. 'I didn't mean Tessa,' he added scornfully. 'She wasn't interested, though I showed it to her.'

She wouldn't be, thought Jo. Not even to be nice to a child. 'Never mind,' she comforted, 'Melanie did, and that's all that matters.'

'She wants one of her own,' Chris replied, ' 'cos I said I'd take mine back to school with me, and that'll only leave her the holidays to look at it in,' he ended somewhat obscurely.

'Get Melanie to buy a different one,' suggested Dan, trying to hide a grin. 'That way, you can swap during the holi-

149

days, and enjoy two books for the price of one, so to speak.'

'I'll tell her, tomorrow.' Chris was enthusiastic. 'It's her pocket money day, so she's bound to go into S̲t Mendoc to the sweet shop.'

'If you go as well, you'll be able to help her choose it,' Dan laughed openly now. 'Have you got any pocket money left?'

'I supply him with all that's necessary.' Jo's voice was quiet, but quite determined.

'I wouldn't try to usurp your authority.' Dan looked at her coolly, his glance level, and now unsmiling.

'Can we go to St Mendoc tomorrow, Jo?' She was glad Chris remembered to ask her, though if they lived there he would have greater freedom, despite treating Penderick House as home he still acted as if they were temporary residents.

'Yes, I've got to go there anyway,' she smiled, and hoped fervently he would not question. 'Have you shown Dan and Lance your bird book yet?' she sidetracked him successfully.

'It's a beauty. It was a Puffin—like that one, look—we brought in this afternoon.' Lance became as absorbed as the child.

'I'm going in again myself in the morning,' Dan told her. 'When Lance wirelessed that he was in trouble I didn't stop to pick up that engine part. It's waiting at the boatyard, so if you'd like a lift?' His tone suggested he did not care either way, and Jo hesitated. She would have liked to refuse, but if the bus was full, and it happened to be wet . . . She bit her lip.

'Can I ride in the front with you this time?' Chris settled the question for her. 'That is, if Hannah isn't coming along too?'

'Best ask your sister.' He didn't even call her by name, thought Jo irritably. 'If she doesn't mind sitting in the back . . .'

'Of course I don't.' It would save her from having to sit by Dan. She felt glad enough to be spared the ordeal, she thought thankfully.

'That's settled, then.' Dan pulled her chair from the table courteously as Hannah brought in the soup.

'I'm making Mr Julian an omelette, miss,' the elderly woman bent over her. 'He's not partial to lobster, and I wondered if you might like one too?'

'May I, Hannah? If it's not too much trouble?' Relief flooded through Jo in a wave. She did not want to refuse the lobster, and thus add fuel to Dan's amusement at her predicament that afternoon. But her tummy felt as if lobster was the last thing it could cope with at the moment. An omelette would be the ideal answer.

'A lot of folk don't like lobster,' Hannah nodded, and went off. Jo did, but she didn't relish the one Dan had caught, she thought mutinously, and she would be long gone from Penderick House before she touched another, and they need never know her partiality. If Dan had been better tempered that afternoon she could have laughed off her malaise and thought no more about it, but she bitterly resented him telling Tessa, handing the girl ammunition for her spite, which she used to good effect.

The warm, light meal helped, she discovered, somewhat surprised that it should be so, but by the time she reached the steamed ginger pudding, that was so light it rivalled the omelette, she already felt well enough to tackle it with gusto. With a cup of coffee in her hand, beside the drawing room fire afterwards, she felt completely recovered. And with her physical troubles settled, her mental ones reasserted themselves. Chris's mention of returning to school made her realise just how little time she really had.

Dan mustn't wait for us tomorrow, she thought worriedly. He mustn't know what I've gone for. She did not want him to know until everything was settled. The words on the torn poster advertising the cottage for sale haunted her mental vision. 'Two rooms up, two down,' it had said. Well, that would be enough for herself and Chris. And she knew just where it was; it stood off the main street on a safe, secure site, that was not likely to deposit itself into the ocean in the middle of the night. True, it hadn't got a garden. A small, lost part of her, that still missed the Oxfordshire countryside, mourned the lack of a garden. But beggars can't be choosers, she told herself firmly. For the foreseeable future at least, so long as she and Chris had an established home she would have to thrust aside personal preferences. Maybe later on ... The insurance on the one cottage would probably go a good way towards paying for the other; the one in the village had looked quite a bit smaller. All she would need then would be a job, and until Chris left school she would make herself content with just paying her way, she told herself firmly. It didn't really matter what sort of job. Maybe the hotel would be able to offer seasonal work? Her mind found the possibility unattractive, but she had to be practical.

'By the way, about the insurance on your cottage.' Julian spoke to her from across the hearth, and she started guiltily. It was almost as if he had read her thoughts. 'It's all but finished, now, except for one minor matter. After that it'll only need your signature, and the insurance company will be able to reimburse you. I'll give you the details after you've seen that young man up to bed, unless you'd planned anything else for this evening?'

'No, I'll be down in a little while. And thank you, Julian.' She escorted Chris upstairs, grateful that she now need not find an excuse to remain up there after she had seen her brother safely to bed. A discussion with Julian on the insurance would be an ideal barrier, she thought thankfully, to prevent her from having to engage in conversation with Dan. Tonight of all nights she wanted to avoid that. She felt angry, resentful—and hurt. And Dan was the cause.

She straightened Chris's clothes, that he had dropped higgledy-piggledy on the floor, and offered him the usual mild scolding he received every night for his carelessness.

'Is your tummy better now, Sis?' Adroitly he parried her homily with a question, and she smiled.

'Yes, but it wasn't funny at the time. Though Tessa seemed to think it was. And Dan.' She still smarted, and although she had not meant to talk about it to the child, the words came out before she could prevent them.

'Dan didn't laugh,' Chris said seriously.

'He must have done. Tessa did, and Dan must have told her the story,' Jo said angrily. 'They were laughing together when they came out of the drawing room after we got back.'

'They were laughing about the couple on the cabin cruiser,' Chris contradicted her. 'I know, 'cos I was on the rug looking at my book when they were talking about it. And he didn't tell Tessa about your tummy. Melanie and me was going to ask you to take us bird spotting later, with the book.' Jo let his grammar go for the moment, she was too interested in what he was saying to correct him. 'An' Dan told us not to bother you 'cos you was poorly, an' Tessa was there an' heard,' he finished adamantly.

So Dan hadn't laughed over it with Tessa. It was only Tessa who had sneered, not Dan. Relief and guilt caught at Jo in about equal proportions, but relief won, and she hung up her brother's jacket without her usual admonishment.

'He only told Hannah about it 'cos he thought lobster might make you feel awful,' Chris added as he snuggled down, and Jo stared at him. So Dan was responsible for the omelette at dinner, too? She felt truly awful now, but it was her conscience, not her tummy, that suffered. She'd been hateful to Dan, and quite unjustly. It was understandable, she mused, for him to be angry when he found they had taken the *Kittiwake*. Fear probably made him angrier than he might otherwise have been, since he was aware, and Lance was not, that the engine was working on the home-made part, and was liable to give way at any moment. She went hot at the thought of what might have happened if the storm had decided to blow up again. And Dan still had to get his engine part. He had abandoned his own plans to come out and tow them back to harbour, and now he had to make another journey the following day.

She re-entered the drawing room with some trepidation. Despite her coming discussion with Julian, she found she did not want to be in close proximity to Dan. He was standing by the coffee tray as she came through the door.

'Hannah's made us some more coffee. Come and indulge,' he invited her.

She looked across at him in surprise, but he continued to calmly pour out, and when he had given her a cup, and taken one for himself, he resumed his seat beside Lance.

'I've brought some of the proposals for the *Gull* from the boatyard. They're purely cosmetic alterations, but I'd like your opinion.' He handed a bundle of technical-looking sketches to his brother, who leafed through them interestedly.

'These look fine,' he nodded. 'Except for this one. Wouldn't it be better to go about it this way, instead?' He pulled a pen from his pocket and made a rough sketch on the back of the paper.

'Those two are deaf to everything when they're talking boats,' Julian smilingly excused their absorption. 'They don't notice whether anybody else is in the room or not.'

And they don't bear malice, either, Jo realised with relief. The thought that she might have been an instrument, however innocent, to bring strife between the two brothers had troubled her, and it was in a happier frame of mind that she settled down to discuss insurance matters with Julian, and the next morning rode in the back seat of Dan's car to St Mendoc, with the comforting knowledge that their now derelict property had been a lot more valuable than she imagined, and she would be well placed to bargain for the cottage in the village high street.

'There's the bus, and Melanie's on it—look!' Chris tumbled out of the car the moment it stopped. 'I told you she'd go to the sweet shop first.'

'Come on then, I'll go with you.' Jo sent him off after Melanie, and turned to Dan. 'We needn't bother you any longer,' she said sweetly. 'You'll be glad to get your engine part, I'm sure.' She did not want him to accompany them. The cottage that was for sale was close to the bookshop, and the notice advertising it said the shopkeeper held the key. She wanted to deal with this herself, she already felt indebted to the Penderick family, and she had no doubt if Julian or Dan knew what she was about they would try to help her. Dan would probably end up by telling her what she must or must not do. Her chin set in a stubborn line. She knew what she wanted to do—move herself and her brother out of Penderick House and into a home of their own. And give herself breathing space to collect her thoughts, she added silently, and sort out her feelings for Dan. Maybe when she was away from him, and did not see him about at all times during the day, her heart might give her a bit of peace. Maybe, even, get over its infatuation, she thought, but she knew, deep down, it was not infatuation, and being apart from him would not alter her feelings.

'Don't let Chris persuade you to buy a book you don't want,' she cautioned Melanie, conscious that the boy's enthusiasm for his hobby might sway the young girl's choice. 'Better leave your toffee sticks until afterwards, if you're going to browse,' she warned them off sticky fingers. 'Take all the time you want, I'll do a bit of browsing of my own.' She wanted a word with the bookseller, out of earshot of the young pair, who might chatter over what they heard.

'Indeed yes, the cottage is for sale.' The man leaned on

the counter, happily prepared for a chat. 'The lady who owns it has gone inland to live with her daughter. Did you want it as a holiday cottage?' he enquired.

'No, I want it as a permanent home,' Jo assured him.

'It's a wee bit on the small side,' the man regarded her doubtfully.

'That's all right, there's only my brother and myself, and Chris is away at school during the term time.'

'In that case, take the key and have a look round. You can bring it back when you want to. In fact I'll come and let you in myself, when I've seen to the needs of these two young people,' as he spotted Melanie and Chris heading towards him.

'Melanie says she knows the cox of the lifeboat,' Chris blurted out with some awe. 'She says we can go and see over it if we want to. Can we, Jo?' he begged.

'Well, if you're sure it's all right?' Jo looked at Melanie for confirmation.

'It is, he said we could go,' the girl nodded.

'In that case go along, and I'll walk down to the lifeboat station in a little while and meet you.' It would occupy the pair nicely while she had a look round the cottage, she thought thankfully.

'I didn't know you knew one another?' The bookseller handed over Melanie's purchase.

'Jo made my pendant. The one I showed you,' Melanie claimed more than acquaintanceship. 'I told you . . .'

'In that case,' the man's face took on a look of interest, 'did you also tell the lady what I asked you to?'

'No, I haven't seen her since,' Melanie replied. 'But you can ask her yourself, now she's here.'

'Ask me what?' Jo was mystified.

'About the pendant,' he began.

'It was one I made myself.' Surely he did not think Melanie had been shoplifting?

'Exactly. I'm told you design the jewellery, and make it yourself.' The shopkeeper looked at her questioningly, seeming to seek confirmation of something.

'That's right. I found this particular stone on the shore, and as I'd got a mount with me I made it up for Melanie.' Jo made it quite clear where the girl had received it from.

'It's beautiful. And good quality, too,' the shopkeeper beamed. 'You've probably seen that we do a small line in gift ware here, all of it high quality.' He waved his hand about the shop. 'But mostly, it's pottery work, and visitors don't always want another pot to add to their collection. Good quality jewellery would sell well,' he said shrewdly. 'Did you make your own brooch yourself?' he fixed interested eyes on the one gracing Jo's jersey.

'Yes, I wanted a fairly plain one . . .'

'It's ideal for the sort of trade we attract,' the man told her. 'Excellent quality, in good taste, without costing the earth—a piece of jewellery like that would make a really nice holiday souvenir without being blatantly "*a present from Blackpool*".' He spoke in italics, and Jo laughed.

'I love the work,' she admitted, 'though I'd never considered doing it on a commercial scale before.' Chris had suggested it, and she had toyed with the idea, but it hardly seemed a feasible means for an income in such a small place.

'We've got another shop at Arlmouth,' the man might have been reading her thoughts. 'Perhaps you'd care to think it over, as you intend to remain in the district,' he suggested. 'I'd be prepared to take all you make of this kind of thing. The pendant, for example, would fetch . . .' He mentioned a price that made Jo's eyebrows rise.

'I had thought of looking for a job to occupy the winter months,' she said tentatively. She did not want her companion to know how her heart thumped with excitement at the prospect. Here was the answer to her problems—a steady income from the sale of her jewellery. A bright smile transformed her face. Work she enjoyed, and a home of her own to do it in. The thought brought her back to the cottage.

'I'll bring in some of my designs to show you,' she offered. 'Some of the matching sets are really very pretty. But now——' she held up the key to remind him.

'Ah yes, the cottage. I'll come and let you in, the lock's a bit stiff.' With olde-worlde courtesy that Jo found very attractive—it reminded her sharply of her father—he handed her out of his own door and armed her along the street. 'There now, I'll leave you to look round on your own. Just close the door and pop in to let me know what you think, when you've finished.' And he left her.

The hall was tiny, the stairs steep. And there were, indeed, two rooms up and two down as the advertisement said, but although the outside of the cottage looked narrow, squeezed in between others along the street, it was surprisingly roomy. It was in good condition as well. If only the price was right ... She sought the bookseller.

'Are any other people interested in the cottage?' She held her breath for his reply. The asking price was several hundred pounds below what she would receive from their previous dwelling, it would leave her a nest egg to lean on as well as something to make the cottage comfortable. Green curtains would look nice ....

'No, there's no one else interested in it, or likely to be,' he set her mind at rest. 'There aren't many people who actually want to settle here to live,' he went on conversationally. 'There's not much choice of work, except for the fisher folk, and mostly people just want to hire a cottage for the summer. And the owner doesn't want to let it, she wants to sell outright and get a lump sum behind her, you understand,' he explained.

Jo understood very well. She felt a bond of sympathy with the unknown owner, who she had elicited was also the widow of a fisherman.

'How can I get in touch with her?' Now she had seen the place she could hardly wait to have the purchase settled, and move in.

'I'll be seeing her myself some time this afternoon, as a matter of fact.' The shopkeeper was eager to be helpful. 'She's by way of being a relative of mine, and we keep in touch. The place is as good as yours,' he assured Jo.

Someone else who's related, she smiled to herself, but she made her way out of the shop with light steps, and more hope in her heart than she had known for several months.

'Hello, Amos,' she called cheerfully across the street to the old fisherman, who was making his way down to where his rowing boat was tied up at the breakwater. The *Sea Swallow* was anchored out in the bay, and Jo could see Roddy already in the row boat waiting for Amos to join him.

'Hello, Amos!'

He heard her. She was certain he heard her. He must have done, for he glanced towards her as she spoke, but instead of replying to her greeting he turned his head away, spat, and carried on walking, ignoring her as if she did not exist.

Jo stopped in her tracks, and the colour drained from her face. What contempt the old man must have for her, to do such a dreadful thing! All her new-found cheerfulness deserted her with a rush, and left her feeling sick. Amos must know she and Lance had taken the *Kittiwake* out, and that Dan had to bring the *Sea Swallow* to rescue them, and this was the old fisherman's reaction. Slowly Jo started to walk towards the lifeboat station. She had hoped to look round it, when she joined Chris and Melanie, but now she no longer wanted to. The lifeboatmen probably held the same low opinion of her; news would travel fast in such a small community, and no doubt Amos had expressed his opinion to his contemporaries in as forceful a manner verbally as he had exhibited by his silence now. Her spirits sank to zero, and she dropped on to the low stone coping of the sea wall and watched listlessly as Amos waded out to Roddy, and the boy began rowing towards the trawler. Was she wise to purchase the cottage in the high street? Or would it be better to go back inland, where she belonged? Where Tessa said she belonged? Her heart cried an anguished 'No!', but her troubled mind filled with doubt.

'I thought you were coming to see over the lifeboat with us.'

'Have a piece of toffee, it's lovely.'

She shook her head, blankly, refusing the toffee. Anything to eat would choke her, she thought miserably.

'I stayed browsing longer than I intended to,' she excused her non-appearance to the ebullient pair. 'Are you two ready to go back to the car? I'll just have to pop back to the bookshop and get a magazine I forgot. You can go on and wait for me.' She would have a word with the shopkeeper, tell him she wanted time to think over the purchase of the cottage. She chose a magazine blindly, to make her excuse true. She would give it to Hannah, the housekeeper would enjoy the knitting pattern that her blurred eyes picked out on the front cover.

'About the cottage...' she began as she paid the proprietor.

'Well now,' the man looked faintly uncomfortable. 'I did say there wasn't anyone else after it, but that wasn't quite right, it seems.' He shifted his gaze uneasily. It rested with obvious relief on another customer who also approached the counter with a magazine in her hand.

'Good morning, Miss Tremayne,' he called, and turned back to Jo. 'There's a gentleman who wants the cottage as well, and he's willing to pay a good price to reserve it,' he tumbled his words out hastily, patently uneasy at his volte-face. 'Though I can't imagine what he can want it for,' he added half to himself, 'with him living up at Penderick

Head it isn't the sort of place I'd have thought he would want for a home.'

'Dan Penderick asked you to reserve it?' Jo faced him furiously, the direct question thrown at him so that he had to answer, and he nodded, unhappily conscious that he had revealed who the second interested party was. And also, by his guilty mien, betrayed that he had been instructed not to reveal the name of that second party.

'What would Dan want with such a place?' she cried furiously. 'I asked for it first. I have a right . . .'

'I'm sorry, miss, but Mr Penderick offered a much higher price,' the shopkeeper began.

A higher price than she could pay. One he knew she could not possibly match, Jo thought bitterly, a flash of intuition telling her that Dan did not intend her to have the cottage. Why? What was it to do with him where she went, or what she bought?

'Maybe he's prepared to pay to keep you out,' Tessa divined her thoughts with unkind accuracy. 'We don't like strangers here,' she added spitefully, and handed over the money for her purchase.

'Now, Miss Tremayne, that's not true,' the shopkeeper began, and looked as unhappy as the foreman had looked the day before.

'If it isn't true, why should Dan be prepared to pay over the odds for a tumbledown old cottage he doesn't need and can't want?' Tessa asked vindictively. 'You might just as well give in and leave,' she swung round on Jo. 'Go back to where you came from.' She looked at Jo's white face staring back at her numbly, saw the hurt in the pansy brown eyes, and her own gleamed triumphantly. 'If Dan's blocked your purchase of this cottage, he'll block any other you try to make the district. He's rich enough to buy half a dozen and not notice,' she persisted spitefully.

'In that case, there's no more to be said. Thank you for

the magazine.' With her head held high Jo nodded to the shopkeeper, and calling up all her pride to aid her dignity she walked past Tessa and quit the shop.

I'll leave Penderick House tomorrow, she vowed. Dan should not have the satisfaction of seeing how his action had hurt. Coming on top of Amos's contemptuous rebuff, it dealt her a blow that left her feeling strangely empty inside, an emptiness that was slowly being filled by a cold, consuming anger. It was a sly, underhand means of getting rid of her, a cowardly means. He must have seen the shopkeeper take her to the cottage, and realised her intention, and then waited until she left before he went to the bookseller himself and told him to stop the purchase. She had no doubt Dan had told the man that, and being a local, he would do as the Pendericks asked, rather than oblige a stranger.

She refused to break the silence between them on the way back. Melanie accompanied them, and scrambled into the back seat with Chris, so that they could open the new book between them and look at it right away. Perforce, Jo had to take the front seat beside Dan.

'Did you get all you wanted in the village?' He looked at her searchingly, and she avoided his eyes.

'No,' she replied curtly. He knew she had not, so why ask, unless he wanted to gloat over foiling her plans?

'Jo . . .' He hesitated, then his glance went to the two youngsters on the back seat, and he shrugged. 'It'll do later,' he said, and lapsed into silence, that became charged with feeling as they took the road towards Penderick Head, but Jo felt disinclined to break it, even though the sense of strain between them became almost unbearable, a tangible presence, like a silent menace, that seemed to destroy her power of speech in the car, and her appetite for the excellent lunch Hannah served shortly afterwards.

'By the way, Miss Jo,' she set down a small, awkwardly

wrapped parcel beside Jo's plate, 'Amos called in half an hour since, and he asked me to give you this, from him, special.' Her eyes smiled.

'From Amos?' What would Amos want to send her? Particularly after their unfortunate meeting that morning. Jo slid aside the paper wrapping wonderingly. 'Why, they're coloured stones. Here's some small ones that match Melanie's pendant. Oh, Hannah, they're lovely!' She trickled the multi-coloured offering through her fingers. 'There's enough to keep me occupied for ages. But why should Amos...?' She raised puzzled eyes to the housekeeper.

'Well, he thought you might be a bit put out by this morning, like,' Hannah said placatingly. 'It's even dawned on Amos that other folk might not understand his odd ways.'

'Understand what?' Dan's voice sounded uncompromising. 'What happened between you and Amos this morning?' he demanded from Jo, and she flushed. It was no concern of Dan's what had happened that morning, and in view of his attitude she felt disinclined to supply him with an answer. She resented his tone, and if he wanted her out of the district anyway, why should he bother if she and Amos had crossed swords? Surely it would suit him if the old fisherman made her feel unwelcome as well?

'Amos met Miss Jo on his way down to the *Sea Swallow* this morning,' Hannah explained for her, and saved Jo from answering. 'He ran out of baccy on his way back from the fishing grounds, so he anchored up in the bay and got Roddy to row him ashore to buy some before he took the boat on into the harbour to unload. You know what he's like for his baccy,' she exclaimed. 'Miss Jo saw him going back to the boat and spoke to him.' She said it as if it was something significant, and Jo wrinkled her brow, feeling lost. Hannah spoke in riddles, and her patience was wearing thin with trying to solve them.

'Of course I spoke to him,' she cried. 'I couldn't just ignore someone I knew, pass them by in the street without a word...'

'Amos and his confounded superstitions!' Dan's voice grated harshly. 'They make him positively uncivilised.' His scowl boded ill for Amos when they met.

'Why, what have I done wrong now?' Would she ever understand these people? Jo wondered despairingly.

'You haven't done anything wrong at all,' Julian butted in, his gentle voice easing both her own annoyance and his brother's black look. 'It's just that—according to Amos's generation—it's unlucky if a woman speaks to a man on his way to his boat. What did he do?' he quizzed Jo kindly. 'It's my guess,' when she shook her head, refusing to reply, 'it's my guess he looked away from you, and spat?' There was a twinkle in his eye as Jo's quick flush proved him right. 'That wasn't intended as an insult to you,' he pointed out. 'It was merely a propitiation to lady luck, that's all.'

'I felt—I felt——' she stammered to a stop. She did not want to explain, not even to Julian, how she felt.

'Upset, I'll warrant,' Hannah looked at her keenly. 'Well, it even penetrated Amos's thick skull that other folk might not like it,' she said grimly. 'Not that it'd bother him with most lassies, but he's got right fond of you,' she added surprisingly.

'Of me?' First Lance had told her, now Hannah. Could they be right? A small warm spot touched her bleak mood at the thought.

'Aye, you,' the housekeeper nodded. 'Why, I mind he even said he hoped—oh well, never mind what he hoped,' Hannah suddenly became over busy with rearranging the plates on the table. 'Anyway,' she threw over her shoulder offhandedly, 'he stopped to pick up some pretty stones out of the cove for you. He heard Melanie say you wanted some for your jewellery,' she finished.

'How kind of him!' Jo's eyes softened at the old man's touching gesture. 'I'll go and thank him right after lunch.'

'You won't see him until tomorrow,' Julian put in. 'I happen to know he's taken the *Sea Swallow* up to Arlmouth, he'll probably trawl his way back, maybe spend the night on the boat.'

'He knows there's no need to bother.' Dan sounded exasperated. 'His catch was more than enough this morning.'

'You know Amos,' Julian shrugged. 'When there's a good shoal running he can't resist them. I've warned him before about wearing himself out, there's no need, the retainer you pay him alone is more than enough to keep him.' He glanced straight at Dan as he spoke and the twinkle in his eye brightened at the sheepish look on his brother's face 'Oh, I know you pay him a pension . . .'

'It's a retainer, not a pension,' Dan growled.

'Call it a pension and Amos would starve rather than accept it,' Julian smiled openly now. 'But he'll never stop fishing, so long as he can take a boat out. He's past it really, but he's nothing if not stubborn.' He shook his head.

'It keeps him happy.' Dan closed the subject with a note of finality, patently uncomfortable by the disclosure of his thoughtful provision for the most senior of his trawler skippers.

Lying awake late that night, Jo wondered what happiness Amos could find, groping through the dark waters, that lay now shrouded in the sudden, treacherous fog that came up suddenly along the coast hereabouts, descending from nowhere in a blinding blanket, and lifting just as unexpectedly. By tomorrow morning it would probably be gone.

She wondered if the young, dark-haired mother-to-be lay listening, as she did, to the eerie hooting of a foghorn from somewhere out beyond the bay. She shivered as she thought of the Claw Rocks, and lay half dozing, half listening.

There seemed to be only the one hooter. Something about the sound seemed vaguely familiar to her dreaming mind. Two short blasts and a long one. Surely Amos had not got his own fog code, as well? It would be just like him, to be different from all the rest. She smiled into the darkness. All the other fog signals she had heard had been one long hoot, at intervals. Two short blasts, and a long one ... It went on and on, like an S.O.S.

An S.O.S. She sat bolt upright in bed, shocked into full wakefulness. That was what it was. The eerie hooting came again. Two short blasts, and a long one. The universal distress signal. And Amos—stubborn old Amos, who was long past his fishing days, but would not give in—was somewhere out there on the *Sea Swallow*. And calling to them through the darkness and the fog, for help.

CHAPTER TEN

'DAN, wake up! Dan!'

Jo hammered on his bedroom door, fear lending strength to her fists. The S.O.S. still echoed through the house, like the sound of doom. It drove her from her bed, heedless of the fact that her nightdress swirled about her feet in a froth of blue nylon and white lace, uncovered by her dressing gown which she ignored in her haste as it hung on the back of her bedroom door, and she fled along the landing to where Dan's room lay at the head of the stairs.

'Dan! Wake up!'

'What on earth's the matter?'

The door opened and Dan stood there. His hair was tousled, one hand rubbing the daze of sleep from his eyes.

'It's Amos,' she stammered incoherently. 'He wants you.'

'Amos is out in the bay, on the *Sea Swallow*. Julian told you,' he towered above her, wide awake himself now. 'You've been dreaming, and it's frightened you.' Almost roughly he reached out and drew her to him. His one hand gripped her round the waist, and the other rose and stroked her hair.

'There's no need to be afraid, darling.' His voice was soft, almost a whisper, and she had to strain to hear. 'Fog doesn't worry Amos, he's been a seaman all his life.' His hand left her hair, and his fingers cradled her chin, tipping her face up to his. 'He'll be all right.'

'But he's not all right.' She choked on the knowledge. Had Dan really called her darling, or was she dreaming, as he said? She looked up into his eyes, the blue, far-seeing eyes of the mariner, that now looked deep into her own with

167

an expression in them that made her heart leap.

'That's his foghorn you can hear now . . .'

'I know. That's what I mean.' She found her voice again. Later, she would remember what he said, would believe it, if she could. But not now. There was no time, now. 'He's calling you with his foghorn, Dan. He needs you.' Was it her imagination, or did the sound of the foghorn falter as they listened?

'I believe you're right.' He cocked his head, taking notice. 'You *are* right.' He straightened away from her abruptly, and cradled in the circle of his arm she felt him stiffen. 'Lance!' He loosed her and spun round, and sprinted for the door at the end of the corridor. 'Lance!' He did not stop to hammer on it as Jo had done on his, but opened it and went straight in. She heard his voice calling to his brother, heard Lance's sleepy answer, then an alert, wakeful response.

'Jo, phone the lifeboat station, will you?' Dan came back to where she still stood outside his door, paused and spoke to her. 'You'll find the number on the pad on the hall table.' He swung back in the act of re-entering his room, and briefly, urgently, caught her to him again, straining her against him with an intensity of feeling that shook him out of his normal self-contained reserve.

'Jo—sweetheart,' his voice was hoarse, hurried with the urgency of the siren upon him, that still called and called. 'We must talk when I come back. Promise me we'll talk?'

Jo nodded, dumbly. She could not reply. Dan bent his head and his lips touched hers in a hard, swift kiss that smothered any response she might have made.

'Get dressed,' he said abruptly, and disappeared himself to do the same.

'I'll dress afterwards.' She paused only to snatch her dressing gown from behind the door and slip it across her shoulders before flying downstairs to the telephone. The number of the lifeboat station was printed in large letters on the pad beside the telephone, along with the numbers of the doctor and the other emergency services. She dialled, and surprisingly her fingers did not tremble. One part of her mind, while acknowledging the crisis, remained icily calm.

'Penderick House here.' She identified herself. 'There's a fog hooter sounding from a trawler. It's sending out an S.O.S.'

'It's just woke me up, missie. I'll set the siren off, and call the crew in right away.' The voice at the other end sounded jerky, as if the man was holding the phone to his ear with one hand, and struggling to get his clothes on with the other.

'He's heard the hooter, he's going to call the crew.' She did not waste time as Dan and Lance appeared fully dressed, and took the stairs three at a time. How did they manage to get dressed so quickly? They must keep a set of seagoing clothes beside their beds, ready for just such an emergency. She learned later that they did. Dan stopped as he reached her side, and bent swiftly towards her.

'Try not to worry. We'll be back,' he promised. His hand touched hers, and for a second her fingers twined about his, clinging, holding him to her, then she let him go, and seconds later the engine of the car burst into life and grew fainter down the drive.

'I'll put the kettle on.'

Jo had not noticed Hannah until now, had not seen that Julian stood beside her in the hall, tall, and seeming to stoop more than ever in his enveloping dressing gown. She pulled her own to, suddenly conscious of her filmy attire.

'I'll come and help you. I'll just look in on Chris first, in case we've disturbed him.' Desperately she wanted something to do, to prevent her mind from thinking. She opened her brother's door and leaned over his bed, but he slept on undisturbed, and looking at him curled into a relaxed ball under the covers she envied him. By the time Chris woke up the fog would most likely be gone, and the saga of the night would be ended. He would not have to endure the hours of waiting, wondering what—if——

'If you're going to wait up, Julian, come and sit by the fire.' She shut her mind resolutely to the whats and ifs, and stirred the still glowing embers on the hearth. She reached behind her to the hod and fed the resulting flame carefully, placing logs with meticulous care crossways one over the other, concentrating all her attention on making the fire burn up so that she should not remember that Dan was driving towards the lifeboat station, along the coast road that dipped and turned on top of the cliffs above the bay, much of it unfenced, and blanketed by the same fog that shrouded the *Sea Swallow*.

'Dan knows every inch of the road, Jo.' Julian's eyes were on her face, reading her thoughts as she knelt on the rug tending the flames. He must have sat through many a vigil like this, Jo thought with sudden compassion. Perhaps longing to go with the other men, but compelled by physical disability to remain at home with the women, and wait. In a way it would be easier to endure the danger than the waiting. That needed a particular kind of courage.

'The lifeboat siren's stopped,' she realised. The fog hooter still sent out its mournful cry for help, but the intervals between the S.O.S. signals seemed longer, now.

'The boat's got its crew,' Julian answered her comment. 'There's no need to keep that racket up when they've got a full crew, it'll only disturb the whole village.'

The practical approach again. Jo marvelled at their outlook, but found herself nodding, appreciating their point of view. There were children in the village who needed sleep; elderly people, and maybe ailing ones as well, and they all had to be considered.

'What a comfort you are, Hannah!' Julian smiled at her kindly as she appeared with a tray of tea.

'It always helps,' she nodded towards the pot and settled herself in the chair on the opposite side of the hearth to him with the accustomed attitude of one who had gone through the same ritual countless times before, and once again prepared herself to wait through the long hours ahead. The clock on the mantelshelf struck the half hour.

'Half past two?' Jo exclaimed. 'It seems a lifetime since we went to bed.'

It would seem another lifetime before it got daylight, she thought, shrinking from what she knew must be a long wait. Thank goodness it got light early, it would have been unbearable if it had been the other end of the year, and daylight tardy in coming.

She took her cup from Hannah, and looked up from where she still sat curled on the rug. She caught the older woman's eyes. Hannah had that special kind of strength. Sudden compunction touched Jo. She herself was afraid, but primarily for Dan. For the others too, of course, but mostly for Dan. And in a way it was a selfish kind of fear. Hannah was equally afraid for them all. Dan and Lance were like sons to her, and she was related to Amos and Roddy. How did she bear it? Impulsively Jo reached out and gripped her hand. It lay limply in the hollow of her lap, making no attempt to raise the comforting cup of tea to her lips, while her faded eyes looked sightlessly into the fire. Remembering the night when she waited in vain for her man to return?

'The boat holed, and sank with all hands . . .'

Hannah's hair lay in a long grey pigtail, neatly plaited down her back. Strangely, the small girl style made her look older than the bun she normally wore it in during the day.

'They're still afloat, or they wouldn't be hooting.'

The tired voice offered Jo comfort in return for her handclasp. Yes, Hannah had that special kind of strength. Would she ever have it? Something like panic touched Jo's hard-won calm. Before tonight—before Dan spoke to her, looked at her in that way—it had been a hypothetical question. Now, she knew, it was one that would have to be answered, and soon. When Dan came back . . .

She must have dozed off. A hammering on the front door woke her, and she stirred stiffly. She should have sat on a chair the same as Hannah and Julian, but the rug had seemed more comfortable. It did not seem so now. Her legs felt stiff, and the back of her neck ached where it had rested on the arm of Hannah's chair.

'It's Dan come back.' She jumped to her feet, and had to grab at the mantel to prevent herself from falling. Her leg had gone to sleep under her, and she rubbed it impatiently, unable for the moment to support herself.

'Dan wouldn't knock on the door.' Julian, for all his limp, was swifter than she was, and he reached the door first.

'Come on in, Ned.' He drew a blue-jerseyed figure into the room. Jo recognised him as one of the lifeboatmen she had seen the other day.

'Dan asked me to come up, Mr Julian.' He put their fears at rest immediately. 'Him an' Lance are staying with Roddy and his ma for a while. There's things to be done . . .' He hesitated, and shot a glance at Hannah.

'Sit down, man, and tell us.' Even now the housekeeper did not lose her calm, though her face looked lined and grey in the faint, early light that filtered through the curtains. 'I'll have to know some time,' she added quietly, 'and I'd just as soon hear it from you as anyone. It's Amos, isn't it?' she guessed.

'Aye.' The newcomer nodded shoberly. 'From what we've managed to get out of Roddy, Amos sent the lad to sleep in the bunk, and decided to sit it out at the wheel himself sooner than bother to come ashore. You know how he was for stopping the night on his boat?'

Even Jo knew that. Amos lived alone, his wife had been dead for some years, and he frequently chose to remain on the *Sea Swallow*—his other love—rather than come ashore to an empty house. Roddy often stayed with him, for company.

'He must've dozed off at the wheel,' the man continued. 'Roddy said he didn't anchor up, he just kept enough way on the boat to steady her against the run of the tide.'

'Was he trawling?'

'No, he'd no nets out. And when he went to sleep he must've slipped against the control and stalled the engine, because she drifted...'

'On to the Claw?' Hannah's words were a long sigh.

'Aye,' Ned nodded. 'The curent took them, and the *Sea Swallow* hit the two end spears of rock broadside on. There's a girt hole in her side, but the rocks held her, she's jammed tight in between the two.'

'Then how...?'

' 'Twas the collision as did it, Mr Julian,' he answered. 'You know the speed of the current there, the boat must have given them rocks a tidy crack. It threw Amos across the wheelhouse, against the bulkhead on the other side. He couldn't have known anything about it, missus,' he offered Hannah what comfort he could. 'He wouldn't have suffered any...'

'What about Roddy?' Hannah did not spare herself.

'Well, the collision shook him straight out of the bunk on to the deck. Being asleep, he had no chance to save himself.'

'What damage?' Hannah waxed impatient, and Jo knew, suddenly, how she felt. Not knowing was worse than knowing.

'Seems as if he's cracked some ribs and hurt his shoulder. He managed to reach the cord that works the fog hooter, but it pained him a lot to pull it. The wireless got damaged in the collision and wouldn't work. He might've given up and waited for daylight if he hadn't been so scared. She started to fill with water, see, as the tide rose. I reckon it'll shift her off the rocks and sink her before it's at the full, and I suppose he thought...' He stopped abruptly, with a look at Julian that clearly begged for help.

'He thought one in a family was enough to die on the Claw.' Hannah finished for him. 'Well, it's had two o' mine now.' With what seemed a tremendous effort of will she gathered herself together and stood up. 'You'll need a cup of tea.'

'Nay, I'll go home to the missus.' The lifeboatman shook his head. 'I only stopped by at home on the way up here, so she'd know where I was. She'll have my breakfast on the stove. Best not let it spoil.' He laid a gnarled hand on Hannah's shoulder for an instant, then with a courteous nod to Julian and Jo he made for the door.

'Take a nip with you, for later.' Jo heard the sideboard door in the dining room open and shut.

'Thank you kindly, Mr Julian. One won't come amiss after this night.'

'The fog's gone.' Julian came back into the room. Going to the window, he drew aside the curtains and let in the welcome light. True to its fickle nature the fog had disappeared, leaving only a faint trace of mist that was clearing even as they looked. From somewhere in the spinney, a thrush started to sing.

'It's another day.' Jo felt numb. What comfort could she offer to Hannah?

'Get dressed, Miss Jo, and we'll put the breakfast on.' Hannah offered Jo a palliative instead.

'I couldn't eat.'

'Maybe not, but the men will need hot food when they come in. And they'll need your strength, too,' she reminded Jo quietly. 'There'll be a lot to do, this day.' Sadly, Hannah knew the routine. 'And there's Chris to see to.' She stirred Jo into action.

'I've made a pot of porridge,' she announced, as Jo reappeared a few minutes later, fully dressed, and having made sure Chris was getting up. 'When you've a job to swallow it slips down easy, and it'll keep you going.' Hannah stirred the mixture with unnecessary vigour. 'Help me to carry the plates through into the dining room.'

'We'll eat in the kitchen this morning, Hannah.' Dan appeared in the doorway, with Lance behind him. 'It's warmer in here, and we can help ourselves from the stove.' His quick glance in Jo's direction told her he did not intend Hannah to be left to eat on her own.

'Am I late?' Chris clattered into the kitchen, and surveyed the assembled grown-ups with surprise. 'What's the matter?' His recent experiences had made him sensitive to atmosphere, and his face took on serious lines.

'One of the trawlers ran into trouble off the Claw during the night.' Dan omitted to tell him which one. 'We had to take the lifeboat out to her.'

'Did you get the crew off?' the boy asked eagerly.

'Yes.' He did not enlarge. 'Come and eat your breakfast now, and I'll tell you about it later, when we're rested.'

'Dan and Lance have been up half the night, don't bother them now, they're very tired.' Dan's face looked haggard and drawn, they both did. Dark stubble showed on his normally clean-shaven chin, and his eyes were weary.

'Sit quiet, and get on with your porridge.' Jo filled more bowls with the creamy brew, smaller ones for Hannah and herself. 'Eat now, it'll warm you.' She gave one each to Dan and Lance, another to Julian. Surprisingly, the tears that in Ned's presence she found difficult to check now did not need to flow. They might later, but for the moment she had work to do. She seated the two tired men into chairs on either side of the hearth, sugared and milked their porridge for them, and pressed them to begin. 'Eat up,' she insisted. 'And Hannah and I will do the same.' She sent them an oblique warning not to let her down, and seating herself beside the housekeeper repeated her advice. In spite of her brave words Hannah found difficulty in following her own advice, but eventually, under Jo's coaxing, she managed the bowl full, and a cup of tea, which Julian thoughtfully laced before she drank it.

'Not for me, thanks.' Dan and Lance both refused whisky in their tea, and Jo shook her head as Julian's hand hovered over her cup.

'Nor me.' She was unaccustomed to drink of any kind, and wanted all her senses alert for the day that lay ahead. It promised to be as long as the night had been. Hannah and the others knew what it would bring, but Jo could only guess. Pain would come, and grieving. For Amos—for Hannah, to whom the fresh wound reopened old ones long healed. And for Roddy, whose ribs would heal but whose mind would bear the scar, as Chris's did, of tragedy endured before his time.

'If you want to go to Roddy's mother, I'll run you there in the car,' Julian offered when Hannah shook her head to Jo's offer of buttered toast.

'She could do with me there, I don't doubt, with young Roddy laid up.' Hannah looked across the table at him. 'But what about here?' She glanced round the kitchen woriedly. 'There's the meals to get, and the shopping and all...'

'I'll cope for you for a few days, until things are more settled.' Jo spoke up immediately, not giving herself time to think. Was today really the day when she planned to move her belongings out of Penderick House for good? She could not have done so, of course, because Dan blocked her purchase of the cottage. Strangely, she had forgotten about the cottage. It was all she could think of yesterday. Now it seemed unimportant beside all that had happened. 'You go and stay with Roddy's mother,' she urged, 'I'll manage until you come back.'

'Go and get your things together, I'll take you straight away.' Julian turned to Jo. 'I'll be away most of the day, I expect. There'll be running about to do, and the car will come in useful.' His clear-thinking ability to organise would be invaluable to the distressed relatives, she knew.

'I'll expect you when I see you,' she removed any difficulties from his path. 'It'll be easy enough to do a quick grill when you do get in. Have you had enough to eat now?' Then as he nodded, 'Just the same I'll put you up a snap.' Unconsciously she borrowed Hannah's terminology. 'You might find it useful during the day.' She knew from bitter experience just how much 'running about' as Julian called it there was to do at such a time, and he might go without food rather than intrude on the bereaved family for meals.

She was glad she had thought of it when Julian did not appear at lunch time, and she turned down the light under the hotpot so that it could go on cooking until Dan and Lance put in an appearance. It did not matter if the meal was eaten at one o'clock or three, she did not intend to disturb them.

'Tell me what happened last night, Sis? It's something awful, isn't it?' Together she and Chris went out to feed the seabirds in the cages, so that Dan should not have to worry about them when he woke. She bent down and scratched the guillemot's neck, talking to the bird rather than to her brother, compassionately turning her back on a ten-year-old boy who was desperately trying to behave like a man.

'It was the *Sea Swallow* . . .' She told him all she knew.

'We can best help by doing the chores here, and keeping out of the way,' she finished quietly. 'They won't want strangers at a time like this. You know how it is?' Chris knew, and so did she. And somehow, during the black days that followed, she coped with running the household for Hannah; supplied meals that were hot and appetising, despite the erratic coming and going of the three men, and now the funeral was over, and Roddy was to be released from hospital within twenty-four hours, Hannah would return on the morrow. And she herself, Jo realised with weary relief, felt tired out, not only from the physical work, but from the nervous strain. She and Dan had not been able to talk, after all. There had been no opportunity for a word alone together, the whole of the week, it seemed, someone or other was there discussing 'the arrangements', as they tactfully put it. Dan and Lance were pallbearers, and out of respect for their feelings Jo put her own to one side for the time being. And now, tomorrow, Hannah would be back and the house would take up its normal routine again. Next week Chris had to travel back to school, and she herself would have to come to a decision.

It seemed a lifetime since they came to stay at Penderick House. The daffodils on the lawns outside told her how the weeks had fled, their shrunken brown heads blew where the once bright blooms had been. Soon the wild pink thrift would carpet the cliffs, from where muffled thuds told her the Council men were heeding Dan's advice and were busy putting a fence round the daffodil field. She would have to start making the bracelet for Melanie. Chris wanted to give it to her as a going-away present. It would be a special one, she decided. Amos had given her those stones ... She filled a jug with water at the sink, and gave Hannah's potted plants a drink.

'Quite the little housewife, aren't you?' She jumped and spun round, spilling some of the water, and Tessa laughed.

'I suppose you thought it was a good opportunity to get your foot in here.' Her suggestion was as unpleasant as it was uncalled-for, and Jo stared at her in silence. The last thing she wanted was a scene with Tessa. There had been trouble enough in the house during the last days, without encouraging more.

'You can't say anything, because it's true.' Tessa misunderstood her silence, and went on vindictively, 'After the way Dan tried to keep you out of the cottage, I'd have thought you'd be only too glad to go.'

'Whatever reason Dan had for reserving the cottage, I'm sure it wasn't to keep me from settling in the district, like you said.' Jo found her voice, and by a great effort of will kept it even. It would be unseemly to shout, now.

'Tell me what other reason there can be,' Tessa sneered. 'You can't!' Her whole bearing challenged Jo to find one.

'I can.' A stern voice from behind them spun both the girls round, and Jo's heart lifted as Dan appeared through the door from the hall. She did not care what Dan's reason might have been, only for the warm, secure feeling that had borne her through the last dreadful week, and sustained her still in the face of Tessa's malice. She and Dan would talk, later. Meantime ...

'I can tell you the real reason. The only reason.' Dan's voice, too, was quiet, and he did not look at Jo, but directly—angrily—at Tessa. 'I reserved that cottage, not to prevent Jo from settling in the district, as you tried to make her think,' he had heard the two girls talking, and his opinion of their visitor was clear on his face. 'I reserved it to try and keep her here—at Penderick House.' He emphasised his meaning.

An early nesting blackbird carolled in the garden outside, and Jo's heart sang with him. It was doubtful if either of her companions heard the song. She stole a glance at Dan's face. It was grim and set. Tessa's had gone white with

anger. And now, briefly, Dan's eyes sought Jo's. They held
the same look of entreaty that had filled them the night of
the S.O.S.

'I wanted you to have time to think—to understand—
what marriage to a seaman could mean,' he said humbly,
his eyes asking her the question that she dreaded, and for
the moment could not answer. He had faith in her strength.
It was she who did not have faith in herself.

'If she's got any sense she'll think twice,' Tessa spat out
furiously. 'A girl wants to be married for keeps, not to have
a few years and then spend the rest of her life as a seaman's
widow, like Hannah, bringing up other people's children, in
someone else's house. It was Hannah I came to see, anyway,' she added, with an attempt at offhandedness that for
the moment made Jo feel almost sorry for her.

'Hannah won't be home until tomorrow.' Unconsciously
Jo called it 'home'.

'What did you want with Hannah?' Dan's voice was curt.

'I've brought the usual flowers for the house, of course.'

'From now on, we won't need them,' he answered her
abruptly.

'But what about my fish?' Tessa looked staggered as the
meaning of his words sank in.

'You'll have to get it from the butcher's, the same as the
other folk in the village do.' The butcher in St Mendoc sold
both meat and fish, the community was too small to support
separate shops, and the men from the trawlers took home
their own.

'Forget what Tessa said,' Jo urged later, after the girl
had gone. She eased her fingers in the handle of the wicker
crate that contained Flippers the guillemot and a number of
the other seabirds that were capable now of fending for
themselves again, and walked beside Dan along the path
towards the end of Penderick Head. She could hear the
guillemot's indignant Unk! at thus being confined.

'It won't be long now,' she sent her voice through the wickerwork to comfort him. 'We're nearly there.' Her feet lagged at the thought. From the end of the Head they would be in full view of the Claw Rocks.

'Couldn't you set the birds free from the beach?' How could Dan bear it? she wondered.

'The birds have a better take-off point from the end of the Head,' he responded. 'If you'd rather not come . . .?' He gave her the opportunity to remain behind.

'I'll come with you.' She could not let him go alone, though she did not want to look when they reached the end of the headland, and the stark, pointed spears of rock came plain into view.

'I thought Ned said the *Sea Swallow* would float off with the tide, and sink?' Surprise conquered her aversion, and she stared uncomprehending at the familiar lines of the trawler, tilted now at a wild angle between two upthrusts of rock, and two more boats, seemingly unharmed, afloat hard by. 'Not two more?' she whispered, horror-struck. Dan had told her it was just the *Sea Swallow* that had foundered.

'No, they're working to salvage the *Sea Swallow*,' he reassured her quickly.

'But what if they foul the rocks, too?' How could he let them risk it?

'There's no danger from the Claw if a boat is under power,' he explained patiently. 'The water's deep there, and they can get close in. It's only if a boat drifts out of control that the current can take it. That's what the *Sea Swallow* did . . .' His face took on grim lines, then cleared, as if with a supreme effort. 'Come, let's loose these birds, before they eat their way out of the basket.' A chorus of impatience drew their attention to their burden, and he lowered the basket on to the sparse turf. 'They've been fed, so they've got nothing to draw them back ashore.'

'Won't they come back when they get hungry?' Jo gave a yearning look at the guillemot.

'No, when they need to feed again, their natural habits will reassert themselves. Within an hour or two they'll forget they've ever been ashore.' He threw up the lid and held the basket slightly tilted to one side. 'Stand clear,' he advised her. 'When they make up their minds, they'll go off in a rush.'

'They don't seem in any hurry.'

'They're only taking stock,' he assured her. 'Wild things don't do anything in a hurry unless they're afraid, and they've learned not to fear us because we've fed them.'

'There goes the gull!' With a peculiar, harsh cry a big blackheaded gull took to its wings. With a wide sweep it soared for a second over the cliff, banked steeply in an air current, and with a wild, laughing chatter it was gone. As if the call had been a signal, the other birds tumbled from the basket, and took to their wings. The guillemot was the last to go. Unable to resist the impulse, Jo reached out to scratch its neck for the last time, but with a quick twist it evaded her hand, and followed the others out over the water.

'Be glad that they're free.' Dan pulled her to him, sensing her need, and with his arm around her she felt happier as they stood and watched their erstwhile charges vanish in different directions as the whim took them.

'I am, but...'

'It's best for them,' Dan insisted. 'They've got their own lives to lead, just the same as we have.'

'Dan, don't heed what Tessa said.' Quickly she turned to face him, her own bleak moment forgotten at the flat, weary sound in his voice. 'She was only being cruel.' She pressed her hands against his shoulders, willing him away from the darkness of the past week.

'The truth is often cruel,' he tightened his grip on her

and drew her slight form to him. 'What Tessa said *was* true, Jo. There's always the risk ... Those trawlers down there—they're not making a film. They're real. Last week was real...'

'I love you.' The words were drawn out of her, and she did not wish them back.

'And I love you. How I love you!' His admission was almost a groan, and she pressed soft palms against his lips, as if by her touch she could still the pain of the sound. 'But you must be sure, Jo. It isn't easy for the women. You've seen—you know——' He caught her hands in his and pressed his lips against her fingers, crushing them in a grip that the force of his feelings made stronger than he realised. She winced at the pain of it, but refused to draw away, grasping the sweet agony of the moment to still the conflict in her heart. If she married Dan, she would have to be strong, for them both.

'I'd leave the sea, if it would make you happier...' He declared the depths of his love by offering to sacrifice that which was life to him.

'No, not that.' Jo shook her head. That was not the way. Better by far to leave him, as Hannah said, than destroy his life.

'Dan! Cooee!' Running footsteps pounded towards them, and skidded to a halt in the shape of Chris, panting from his run. 'Lance says will you come?' He gulped a lungful of much needed air, and went on excitedly, 'There's a marine Sir something or other come to see you. He said it was about the *Gull*.'

'He's a marine surveyor, not a knight of the realm,' Dan laughed, and the tension between them was broken. 'I'd forgotten about him. And Lance had too, I reckon.'

'Is something wrong with the *Gull*?' Don't let anything else go wrong this week, Jo begged silently.

'No, the marine surveyors attend the trials of a new

vessel. We made the appointment to see him a couple of weeks back.'

'You go on and see him, Chris and I'll bring the basket back,' she offered.

'There's no need, Lance followed me.' Chris pointed back towards the house, where a tall, balding man who did not look in the least nautical walked beside Lance towards them.

'Hello, Mr Chataway.' Dan shook hands in a friendly fashion with the newcomer, and apologised ruefully. 'Sorry I was out, I'm afraid it slipped my mind we'd asked you to call.'

'It's understandable in the circumstances.' A pair of kindly grey eyes smiled a greeting at Jo, and she went pink, not sure what he meant by 'the circumstances'. No doubt he meant the trauma of the week just gone, but there was a twinkle hidden in his look that might have meant something else.

'You really don't need to see me about the *Gull*.' Dan spoke again and diverted his attention. 'The boat has been built for Lance here. He'll be the owner and the master. It'll be Lance who'll take her on her maiden voyage, and attend to her trials.' He looked directly across at Lance, watched incredulity dawn, and astounded disbelief.

'Dan, you can't mean ... a brand new trawler ... I thought she'd be yours?'

'I told you, the *Kittiwake* is my boat,' Dan retorted. 'I had her from new, the same as you'll have the *Gull*. It's good for a boat to know only one master, it makes her—sort of—special,' he admitted.

'Yippee!' Lance let out a whoop and grabbed Chris. He swung the boy off his feet in an excess of exuberance, and Jo smiled. His unrestrained joy did not seem amiss, even with the *Sea Swallow* caught on the rocks below. Amos would understand.

'You'll launch her, won't you, Jo? I asked you before, but I didn't know she was mine, then.'

'Yes, I'll launch her for you. But it'll have to be with real champagne, mind.'

'I'll see to it,' he promised with a delighted grin, and he was as good as his word.

Jo felt a flash of pride as she surveyed the *Gull* a couple of weeks later, resplendent in new paint, and waiting like a leashed hound, impatient to be gone from the slips to her own true element. She was not a big, important liner. Just a small trawler, off to begin her trials that would confirm her fitness to join the others in the fleet, but Jo felt deeply involved in a way that she would not have believed possible a short time ago. She had seen the vessel built, almost from the start, and watched it grow. For the first time she really understood Dan's love for the *Kittiwake*. Understood, and shared it.

There was no civic dignitary in the crowd who watched, just the folk of St Mendoc, and Jo did not feel at all shy. She was one of them now. She had shared their sorrow, and now she shared their joy.

'Will you come with me?' Lance generously asked Dan to share the first trip.

'No, I'll stay with Jo, and see your boat's properly launched.' As generously Dan refused. 'Take Chris if you like, it'll be his last chance of a run in her before school tomorrow. We'll come another day—as passengers,' he smiled.

'I'll crew with Roddy,' the boy said promptly. Lance had signed Roddy on as crew, encouraging the boy's wish to go straight back to sea the moment his injuries had healed, and Jo could see Hannah's point when she said, 'Let the lad go, the sea's his life too.' A few weeks ago she would not have shared the housekeeper's view. Now—she understood.

'Will it break first time, do you think?' she whispered her panic to Dan as he stood beside her, and she held the bottle of champagne attached to a long cord.

'Swing it hard,' he urged. 'It's extra good luck if it breaks clean.' She looked up at him swiftly, but now was not the time to tease about being superstitious. They could all do with a bit of extra luck.

'Swing it with me, then, to make sure.'

His hands closed round hers on the glass neck lending his strength to her own as the bottle flew.

'I name this boat the *Gull*. May God bless her, and all who sail in her.' Her voice rang clear and strong on the familiar words. It was the voice of a person who was completely sure of herself, and the man who stood with his one hand on her shoulder, warmly close. It was the voice of someone who had come to a decision, and knew it to be the right one.

The bottle exploded in frothy rivulets, and the *Gull* started to slip slowly away from them. It gathered momentum, and rushed towards the water with an eagerness that made it seem alive. No doubt it seemed so to Lance.

Slowly the crowd broke up into small chattering knots of people and began to disperse, and Jo and Dan were alone.

'Let's walk home along the creek path.' That was where she had first met Dan. It seemed fitting that he should hear what she had to say now, in the same spot.

'It was a good launching.'

They left the beach, with its crumbled debris of what was once the cottage garden. Jo spared it hardly a glance, it was not important now. A heron rose on slow flapping wings from further along the creek, disturbed by their unexpected appearance, and she suddenly chuckled, thinking of the other heron, and her first meeting with Dan.

'It's not my fault he's flown away this time,' she turned

laughing eyes to her companion. 'You've disturbed him as much as I have.'

'Don't laugh at me, you little witch!' He reached out for her playfully, and she turned to run, but he caught her up and held her by her hands, preventing her escape. With strong but gentle fingers he held her at arm's length, looking at her with blue eyes that were dark now with longing which he refused to voice. He had given her time to think over what he said, and staunchly he kept to his part of the bargain.

'You broke that champagne bottle over the *Gull* as to the manner born.' His voice was deliberately light, teasing her.

'I wish Amos could have been there.' She caught her breath on a sharp sigh.

'Don't grieve for Amos, Jo.' Serious now, he pulled her closer, but still he did not take her in his arms. 'He went the way he would have wanted to remember. At sea, and on his own ship. Amos has reached his harbour,' he said gently.

'And I've reached mine.' Sure of her way at last, she homed to his arms, that opened to receive her, and closed about her, like the arms of the harbour, safe and warm and strong. She raised her lips to his, sweetly offering him the answer he longed for, and he bent his head above her, folding her close to him in a way that said he would never let her go.

Long minutes passed, and the silence of the creek lapped round them both, so deep that the heron returned unnoticed, to fish among the shallows, thinking itself alone.

Harlequin

COLLECTION
EDITIONS OF 1978

Harlequin's Collection 1... 1.25

ANDREA BLAKE
Night of the Hurrica...

Harlequin's Collection 106 1.25

ANNE WEALE
If This Is Love

**50 great stories
of special beauty
and significance**

$1.25
each novel

In 1976 we introduced the first 100 Harlequin Collections—a selection of titles chosen from our best sellers of the past 20 years. This series, a trip down memory lane, proved how great romantic fiction can be timeless and appealing from generation to generation. The theme of love and romance is eternal, and, when placed in the hands of talented, creative, authors whose true gift lies in their ability to write from the heart, the stories reach a special level of brilliance that the passage of time cannot dim. Like a treasured heirloom, an antique of superb craftsmanship, a beautiful gift from someone loved—these stories too, have a special significance that transcends the ordinary. **$1.25 each novel**

Here are your 1978
Harlequin Collection Editions...

102 Then Come Kiss Me
MARY BURCHELL (#422)

103 It's Wise to Forget
ELIZABETH HOY (#507)

104 The Gated Road
JEAN S. MACLEOD (#547)

105 The Enchanting Island
KATHRYN BLAIR (#766)

106 If This is Love
ANNE WEALE (#798)

107 Love is Forever
BARBARA ROWAN (#799)

108 Amber Five
BETTY BEATY (#824)

109 The Dream and the Dancer
ELEANOR FARNES (#912)

110 Dear Intruder
JANE ARBOR (#919)

111 The Garden of Don José
ROSE BURGHLEY (#928)

112 Bride in Flight
ESSIE SUMMERS (#913)

113 Tiger Hall
ESTHER WYNDHAM (#936)

114 The Enchanted Trap
KATE STARR (#951)

115 A Cottage in Spain
ROSALIND BRETT (#952)

116 Nurse Madeline of Eden Grove
MARJORIE NORRELL (#962)

117 Came a Stranger
CELINE CONWAY (#965)

118 The Wings of the Morning
SUSAN BARRIE (#967)

119 Time of Grace
SARA SEALE (#973)

120 The Night of the Hurricane
ANDREA BLAKE (#974)

121 Flamingoes on the Lake
ISOBEL CHACE (#976)

122 Moon Over Africa
PAMELA KENT (#983)

123 Island in the Dawn
AVERIL IVES (#984)

124 Lady in Harley Street
ANNE VINTON (#985)

125 Play the Tune Softly
AMANDA DOYLE (#1116)

126 Will You Surrender?
JOYCE DINGWELL (#1179)

127 Towards the Dawn
JANE ARBOR (#474)

128 Love is my Reason
MARY BURCHELL (#494)

129 Strange Recompense
CATHERINE AIRLIE (#511)

130 White Hunter
ELIZABETH HOY (#577)

131 Gone Away
MARJORIE MOORE (#659)

132 Flower for a Bride
BARBARA ROWAN (#845)

133 Desert Doorway
PAMELA KENT (#909)

134 My Dear Cousin
CELINE CONWAY (#934)

135 A House for Sharing
ISOBEL CHACE (#935)

136 The House by the Lake
ELEANOR FARNES (#942)

137 Whisper of Doubt
ANDREA BLAKE (#944)

138 Islands of Summer
ANNE WEALE (#948)

139 The Third Uncle
SARA SEALE (#949)

140 Young Bar
JANE FRAZER (#958)

141 Crane Castle
JEAN S. MACLEOD (#966)

142 Sweet Brenda
PENELOPE WALSH (#968)

143 Barbary Moon
KATHRYN BLAIR (#972)

144 Hotel Mirador
ROSALIND BRETT (#989)

145 Castle Thunderbird
SUSAN BARRIE (#997)

146 Magic Symphony
ELEANOR FARNES (#998)

147 A Change for Clancy
AMANDA DOYLE (#1085)

148 Thank you, Nurse Conway
MARJORIE NORRELL (#1097)

149 Postscript to Yesterday
ESSIE SUMMERS (#1119)

150 Love in the Wilderness
DOROTHY RIVERS (#1163)

151 A Taste for Love
JOYCE DINGWELL (#1229)

Original Harlequin Romance numbers in brackets